Gulf Coast Stories

Journeys Away from the Beaches

by

John Aalborg

JOHN AALBORG

GULF COAST STORIES

First Print Edition

ISBN: 978-0-9849365-0-2

Bleep-Free Press

http://bleepfreepress.com

Cover: "Drift Dolls" by Wolfgang Brinck

All characters in this book are fictional, but Florida USA is, in fact, real.

If Raymond Chandler and Ernest Hemingway had a baby, it would be this great collection of short stories. Witty, gritty, hard hitting and great fun. Vivid and so very real.

Perry Gamsby, Publisher,

StreetWise Publications

Sydney AU

TABLE OF CONTENTS

Furby Mountain Florida — 95

On the day after he receives seriously bad news, a truck driver is invited to ride along with a garbage hauler who wants to take the man's mind off his troubles and see life in a different way. A hungry little Furby does his sweet part.

Exile — 111

Carlos looked at the blackened area, barely noticeable now and covered with wild ferns. Harry said, "She burned it down." Thus begins the quest by a 14-year-old illegal and his sister to solve the mystery surrounding the middle-aged American who has befriended them.

Bible School Tattoo — 123

Paula has been eyeing the empty, prime real estate on my forehead. She wants to tattoo God's phone number on it. A seasoned tattoo artist and his atheist girlfriend ink a Christian girl.

I ate between battles,
I slept among murderers,
I was careless in loving and
I looked upon nature without patience.
Thus the time passed which was given
me on earth.

-- Brecht

Morton's Fork Crossing

Bull Schaffner brushed a hand over his tanned, crew-cut head as he slowed the big semi down and dropped a gear on the approach to Morton's Fork Crossing. Fifty miles inland north of Florida's "Emerald Coast" with the empty, flatbed trailer bouncing along in the narrow, blacktop, county road. *Locals call it Moe's Crossroads* was written on the faxed, hand-drawn map on the passenger seat. Ten minutes earlier a well-dressed, old stranger standing beside his mailbox had helped to interpret the map, and sparked Bull's interest.

"That old gas station at the crossroads. A chick lives there now."

"A chick...."

"First time I saw her I went right through the stop sign."

"Ever see a big eighteen parked there?"

"You can't park there. The people in the big house next door put up posts all along the shoulder. I think they also own the station property. Converted it to an apartment. The girl probably works off the rent."

"You think? So what's she look like?"

The gentleman had put an arm around Bull's meaty shoulder. "I thought you'd never ask."

Now Bull could see the metal posts up ahead, protecting both shoulders of the road all the way to the intersection, with a hand-painted "NO SEMIS" sign fitting right in with the decor. Grinning suddenly, Bull eased his seventy feet of truck close to the posts on the right-hand side and pulled the air-brakes with a loud hiss when he was even with the red-brick house. It was set well back, with a weedy lot separating the immaculate yard from the unkempt building at the intersection. After setting the 4-way flashers, Bull eased himself down the three steps to the ground from the Peterbilt, on the road side, and half expected to hear someone holler. Nothing but the faithful idling of the big diesel which kept the AC running and the inside of the cab and sleeper popsicle cool.

So quiet here in the summer heat — no traffic, not even a dog barking — and the walk over to the converted, old-timey gas-station at the corner was short but the blacktop hot on the soles of Bull's worn, black, Reebok originals. No sign of life there, either, and the vintage Firebird crudely depicted on the map was gone, *old F Bird* penciled in, the concrete blocks where it had been jacked up crumbled and broken, like something huge had run over them. The posts blocking any parking larger than a small car continued around the corner and Bull walked between them and over the concrete islands where the gas pumps had been. Draperies were drawn over the building's two, large, front windows, and the glass was festooned with duct tape laid on in X's for hurricane protection. Patting the .22 Beretta in his right-front pocket — his light-duty arm — Bull raised a fist to rap on the door. The door glass had been replaced with cheap plywood, and he hesitated for a moment as an old, battered pickup truck slowed, made the corner, and went on down the way Bull had come. When it was quiet again, he knocked. Nothing. The numbers on the ratty mailbox next to the road were correct, but ...

"Okay...." Bull frequently conversed with himself aloud, as many truckers do from a life so often spent in a solitary cab. He chanced a more vigorous rap on the door and to his dismay it popped open and swung wide, woofing-out sweet-smelling, cool air. Inside was a large, single room, surprisingly well-furnished, with thick carpeting and tapestries on the walls, a brass bed in a far corner and a kitchenette in the other. "No dirty dishes in the sink? No bathroom?" Backing away, he had to give the door a good jerk to re-close it. "Time to see the piggy in the brick house the wolf couldn't blow down!" Bull laughed.

"Lawn needs cutting," Bull threading his way through a huge installation of plastic playground crap on the way back to the house. "Why do people have kids?" He spied a pile of fairly fresh dog shit and stepped around it. "Dogs I can understand. You have a kid and before you get home from the hospital they want you to start a college fund! Then you gotta register 'em for school and stuff and get their shots....

Can't smack 'em when they're bad, can't take 'em in your car without strapping them down or encasing them in foam.... They come home from school sick and pass the germs on to you.... Soon as they can read they want their own cell phone! Then they want their own car! Then they want, they want, they want ..."

"You talking to me?"

Bull lowered the hand he was about to knock with, the doorway now open and filled with a vaguely attractive, western-styled, thirty-something woman looked like she had just dismounted from a show horse if it weren't for the baseball bat in her hand. Ironed jeans, pointy boots, a burgundy western-cut shirt with pearly buttons.

"Um...." Bull tried to think, but accidentally let go a burp instead.

She stared at him, steel gray eyes too close together. Plucked eyebrows. Two, short, dyed-red braids sticking out sideways over her ears like a younger woman might wear. "Blueberry muffins?"

"Um, yeah!" Bull stepped back. "I'm, uh, looking for the woman lives next door. Or the truck driver who stops by sometimes."

"Which one?"

"Truck driver? His name is Danny. Nice looking guy, red tractor...."

The lady lowered her shoulders and stared into Bull's eyes so intently he could feel heat. "My husband is missing. I filed a report on him three days ago. Bitch next door says her boyfriend's missing, too. I said, you file a report? She says, no, he's a truck driver, he could be anywhere. Mostly gone, she said."

"Right. Um...."

"And you are...?

"Bull Schaffner. I'm a private investigator for McKay Trucking."

The lady seemed to relax a little. "P.I.? Uh-huh. That makes you a corporate investigator, seems to me. You don't look either one."

"Yeah, well.... I need to know if you think the lady next door will be back soon. Or if she has a name and phone number. Stuff like that. Where your kids? Where's the dog?"

"Where's D. B. Cooper? The kids are staying with granny, and they took the dog, and I'm here all alone and it's wonderful. Now git!"

"D. B. Cooper, ha ha. Funny."

She smiled but it was so brief Bull couldn't be sure. "The bitch owes two month's rent so Billy — that's my old man — he tells me this time he's going to boot her out so he goes over there and comes back an hour later with a cud of excuses and no money. He's afraid of her but that little heifer doesn't scare me. Anyway, that night her trucker boyfriend pulls up, which really tees Billy off, you guys always leave the engine idling, and he goes out there and comes back five minutes later all banged up, and, I mean, let me tell you, Billy's twice as big as that Danny of yours,

I've seen him, and then the truck pulls out. Billy said both of them jumped on him. Next day he gets in his pickup to go get feed for the horses and that's the last I seen of him. Now git!"

"The horses hungry?"

"They're eating blueberry muffins. Off the vine." The lady raised her ball bat. "Your eighteen-wheeler better be gone when Billy gets back."

"Why would he want to come back?"

The bat leveled to horizontal and Bull barely dodged a good thrust. He took a step sideways and headed for his truck. Half-way there he turned and looked up at the clear, burning-hot sky. The woman was still in the doorway in a wide stance, the ball bat resting on a shoulder. Bull said, "Think it'll rain?"

§

According to the paperwork, Danny's load was epoxy resin in one gallon, unlabelled cans destined for a distributor at the Port of Houston. The weight on those totaled 30,000 pounds, and at the top of the load was a consignment of 2-cycle, gasoline-powered motorbikes, also headed to a dock in Houston, made in Poland and painted either bright red or bright blue according to the manifest. These would have to be unloaded by hand. *Jeez....* The moped pickup had been in Jacksonville, which explained how Danny could stop and see his girlfriend, who supposedly lived next door here, without going out of route. *Okay....* Bull was mulling this information over as he hesitated, once again, at the front door of the converted gas-station. He was about to decide to pop in and lie down on the bed and wait. The hell with his truck blocking a lane out there, or the impropriety of inviting himself in to this apartment. He knew almost every county cop in the area — he had grown up not far from here — and with his parent's place so close by.... Hey, he could park the rig there and borrow Dad's pickup! "Yup, borrow Dad's pickup," Bull said aloud, but just as he reached the door of his cab a tough-looking teenager or whatever buzzed past him on a bright-red motor-bike, didn't even slow for the stop sign.

"Hey!"

The kid disappeared around the corner. "Not much chance of catching up with that." Just then it came buzzing back alongside another one, this one bright blue, with a big, buxom girl on it, she nearly grazing Bull as they flew past. The 2-cycle engines sounded like hornets, and Bull was momentarily paralyzed for what to do, one hand up on the grab bar of his truck cab. He pictured them coming back and him jumping out to block them. He pictured them all going down into a pile, and them hollering at him what's your problem and he yelling where'd you get those bikes, and as Bull was thinking all this he could hear them again, getting closer, coming back, *they must live around here*, and he jumped out to stop them but stumbled and, just as he had pictured, they all went down in a pile.

The young man was first up and the big girl —
short, blond hair, T-shirt said "Pork out at PORKY'S"
— was just sitting there on the shoulder, her legs
straight out in front of her like a rag doll. Her bike was
still running, on it's side, the rear wheel turning, but
the boy's had quit and was stuck up against one of the
steel posts. Bull saw that the kid had bloody scratches
on the palms of his hands and one forearm, but just as
Bull was about to apologize or something the boy said,
"Sorry, Mister."

"We better get going," the girl said, still sitting
there, looking at her own, scraped forearm.

Bull had gotten to his feet in a kind of crouch,
ready to fend off the rough-looking boy if he got
nasty. "Where'd you get the mopeds?"

"Mopeds?"

"Motor bikes!" the girl hollered, sitting there.

Her bike puttered to a halt, and in the silence Bull
heard another vehicle approaching. It was that ratty-
old pickup he had seen earlier, coming back. It slowed
and screeched to a halt, then inched forward between
the two downed machines and stopped when the
tailgate was even up. A man Bull's age eased on down
to the pavement, in overalls, work-boots, and a one-
size-fits-all baseball cap. The hat was a stained white,
with "CHUD'S" in red letters across the front. His face
was gaunt and covered with beard stubble, but his
arms bulged working-man muscle. He took a look at

Bull, spit, and turned to the girl. "You all right, Missy?"

"Yessir, I think so." She heaved herself up and pulled her shorts out of her crevasses.

The man went immediately to the red moped, easily lifted it, and plunked it into the back of the pickup where it lay bent and nestled amongst a dirty, white-plastic cooler and a flotsam of empty oil and beer cans. Bull felt anger welling up, a condition which could plague him without warning and often without sufficient cause. The man looked at Bull briefly on his way to the other moped, but did not say a word. He did make a point, though, of how light the machine he was lifting was to a man like himself. Tailgate up.

Bull was no posie picker either, and he got right behind the man as the second machine slammed on top of the first. "You got a title for those things? They look new."

The guy turned, and Bull could feel his hot breath waft past, smelled like a burnt electrical socket.

Bull said, "They look too new to be slamming 'em around like that. Must not have cost you much."

The man sidestepped Bull and motioned the girl to get in the back of the truck. Her effort was not a pretty sight and despite himself Bull had to look away. But only for a second. Out of nowhere, it seemed, a young woman was running up to them in the middle of the road, coming up on them fast. Small, barefoot, lavender short-shorts, and a tiny tube-top jouncing from side-to-side. A single, pitch-black braid looked like three feet long was trailing behind her in the wind. Bull's heart pounded up and he stood frozen in awe as her last, long stride picked her up and landed her tanned, bare feet slap in front of CHUD's work-boots, her face inches below his chin. For the first time, the man showed fear, and he backed away a step.

"What did I tell you?" she said, loudly but not at all screaming. "I told you I'd kill you if I caught you hanging around my place again. What is it you don't understand? You think Paradise is waiting with a mansion just for you?"

Watching this from behind, Bull was towering over her with his body still locked in amazement. Not even a hundred pounds, he guessed, yet the kids in the back of the pickup were inching their way back, not looking at all sure of their fate. The man took another step back. "I was just... They wuz'n accident an' I wuz ..."

"Shut up!" The gamine's fists were resting on her hips, her torso leaning forward. The silence which followed was so thick and humid you could feel it, and Bull sucked in a deep breath. There was time enough for him to note that her braid reached all the way down to a chunky-little, perfect ass, and there was a red ribbon at the end. Bull sucked in another breath. His heart was settling down enough for him to resume thinking again, although still engaged with some

primeval instincts. Trouble, he knew. A female to kill
for, he thought. "You have enough problems," a small
voice in his head squeaked. "You have ladies waiting
you don't even have time for. Leave this one be. Don't
pay this one any mind."

Right.

She swiveled around and looked up at him, her
gleaming teeth exploding into a smile. "Who are you?"

Bull swallowed. Her lips were full and painted
vampire red. Large, white teeth that could split bones
for the marrow, and the tip of her tongue darting out
between them like a snake and then she was back at
the motley pickup-truck gang. "Git!"

The CHUD'S man, slumped now, turned and
crawled into the cab of the vehicle. The kids looked
out the sides as the engine cranked up and the entire
mess clattered to the corner, stopped at the stop sign
this time, and began a turn to the right.

Bull came to his senses. "Hey!" he hollered.
"Stop!" He ran a few steps after them.

"I know where they live," the girl said. "I'll show
you later. They call me Monkey."

"Later?" He eased on up to her, but not too close.
She looked Mexican, no, that wasn't good enough.
Aztec? Basque? A space alien? Eyes almost black with
flecks of gold. "Bull Schaffner," he said, swallowing
again. "You are the most, the most, the most fantastic
woman I've ever seen." He had come within a red
goat-hair of saying girl instead of woman.

"Tell me something I don't know."

They were standing in the middle of the highway. Bull sweating some but the girl looked cool, and she had just been running! Plus the pavement must be burning her feet. "Alien," Bull said. "From Spain."

"Ha ha, no, born here." Grinning, a peculiar curl at the corners of her mouth, she turned away from looking at Bull's big, long, shiny rig, and waved a tanned, peach-fuzz arm toward the converted gas station. "You been inside yet?" A hint of a mustache that had never seen a razor.

"Um...."

"Come on." Her voice was special, also. Low and deep, like an older woman after a lifetime of drinking whiskey every night. "I could rent a better place but then I'd have to get a job," she said, and pulled him inside by the wrist and flipped a light switch. Properly furnished for such a dump on the outside. Modern, expensive, and there was a bath area, no walls, with a tub and sink and commode, in the corner behind the door. She went to the fridge. "Ice-water or beer?"

Bull needed a beer bad.

She handed him a Corona after twisting off the cap with a bare hand. "I'll show you how I do that later."

"Later...."

She had perched on one arm of the leather sofa with her own beer, and Bull plunked deep-down into the other end. "So how do you get all this good stuff then?"

"People give me stuff. You looking for Danny?"

"Men give you stuff."

"Right." Her expression soured.

"When you saw him last, was he bob-tailing?"

"No, he had his trailer. My landlord, the guy in the house next door, tried to run him off but we beat his ass, and when Danny got back in his rig I thought he was just going to park it somewhere — he keeps a bicycle chained behind the tractor — but we didn't discuss it first and I remembered he said when he stopped he didn't have much time. He never has time for me, and I think he's married. You married? He had an appointment for a drop in Houston and that's a long, long way from Florida! Oh, you would know that, I'm sure, and when he didn't show up later on the bike I figured he was gone and anyway he promised to pick me up on the way back because he had a load scheduled the other way, well, he's promised to take me along before, never happened ..." (She stopped talking long enough to slug down a long swallow of beer) "... and that's when I was supposed to have everything all settled here so I could lock up and go with him on the road but now after what we did to my landlord, if he doesn't kick me out his old lady will and, so I figure I need to rent a storeroom somewhere for all my stuff first ..." (another slug of beer—god she was beautiful—and that voice!) "... like, right away, and, you know, Danny is gorgeous, he is so fine! Plus he's a good man, and interesting, and he knows so much stuff! I have never! But married, yah, you can tell. Anyway, my landlord is soooo jealous about Danny so I figure he is totally in a wad right now and ..."

"Hold on! " Bull said. "Hold on a minute."

"Okay, but you should know that my landlady reported him missing, I mean, to the police. I mean, she reported her husband missing."

Bull choked back telling her he was also married, and watched her take a sip, then another, those beautiful, sucky lips.... "I, uh...."

"You love me?"

pause.... "Yes."

"You'll get over it."

Another, longer pause. A silence. Both of them sipping on their beers. Both of them with their eyes right on each other. Finally, she said, "They said they were sending somebody. Your company. Your boss got me on the phone. She described you perfectly."

"Great."

"No, she was very complimentary. Aren't you supposed to ask me stuff?"

Bull tried his best to keep his eyes off her points. None of that sports-bra stuff with this girl. "Monkey?"

"My CB handle. My trucker handle. My father was a flatbed driver, and he took me along with him summers when school was out. I used to help him with chaining down loads and stuff. Mostly local lumber loads. I had my own cheater pipe for the strap ratchets — I still have it — and the other truckers used to clap their hands when I'd be hanging from it and get another click. Because I don't weigh much. Danny promised me he'd run flatbeds if I'd go with him. He said he wants to marry me, yeah, right. I miss the road, so I almost said yes. Not about marrying him. Absolute yes about hitting the road with him."

"As you can see, I run a flatbed."

"Yah, yah.... But you're not as pretty as Danny."

"Yah yah." Another long silence, then Bull said, "Did you see Danny's load?"

"Nope. No idea."

"Half of it was mopeds. Some red, some blue. I think we were looking at two of them a few minutes ago."

"Ohhhh...." Monkey chug-a-lugged the rest of her beer and hopped to her feet. Her feet were cute and small and tanned with squared-off toes, the nails painted blood red. Toes he would give anything to taste. He thought she was going to get him up so they could find the kids and the pickup but she plunked down next to him. "Please, please help me find Danny," she said. "But if we don't, well...."

Bull was in love. Again. Only this time it was terminal. This time, he thought, he was going to have to die.

"You need the bathroom before we go?" she said, and handed him back his .22 Beretta.

"How'd you get that?"

"It was in your pocket! Easy. I'll wait for you outside."

She had been close enough — he had felt or imagined the heat of her bare leg through his jeans — but snicking that gun out of his front pocket?

"Trouble," the little voice in his head said.

When Bull made it outside, Monkey was sitting cross-legged on the hot hood of his tractor, a bottle of Windex in one hand and a wad of paper towels in the other. Items he kept in the passenger-side tool box. *That metal must be hot enough to burn a devil,* Bull thought. *I should just shoot myself while I have a chance.* What a sight, though, her arms flying over the windshield, that braid swinging to-and-fro off a shoulder.

§

"Steerage passenger with a deck chair," Monkey said, her bare feet up against the passenger-side windshield. Bull had just made the right turn which the old pickup had made and Monkey told him to go about a mile and there would be a dirt-road turn-off on the left. By the time Bull had gone up through the gears there it was, and he had to hit the brakes hard, his eyes on the mirrors to make sure the empty trailer wasn't jack-knifing.

"You said a mile."

"Seemed like a mile to me," Monkey said.

"Maybe it's your perfume, making me stupid."

"No perfume. I shampooed my hair last night."

Bull swung wide to make sure the trailer tandems didn't drop down into the ditch while visions of Monkey shampooing her hair danced in his head. Halfway into the turn, however, he stopped. The big Caterpillar engine dropped down to it's faithful, boss-man idle. Bull said, "This clay road is too narrow. We gonna be able to turn around down there? And what if a car or a garbage truck comes the other way?" Bull could hear himself sounding indecisive and wimpy, but he had been on country roads like this before and gotten twisted up so badly he had to back up for miles, not an easy task with a trailer. "You think we can..."

The girl dropped her feet to the floor and leaned over and planted a kiss on his cheek. "There. All better."

"Right." Bull made it sound like a grump but after dropping down into 2nd they were off again and roaring up through gears down the red-clay road. A logged-over, new forest was crowding both sides, and the ditches were deep enough to flip a big rig if Bull wasn't careful. But hey, he was feeling alive, and pumped, and young!

I know she's playing me....

He slowed for a gentle bend up ahead — you could not see around it for the new growth — and half way through a woman wearing a kelly-green babushka with a little kid in a back-pack came buzzing right at them. The child was poking his head out, the two of them on a shiny-new, blue moped. In a heartbeat the woman corrected her path just in time and without slowing down she made it around them, her face twisted in surprise, the kid sucking a thumb.

Bull hit the brakes. "You see that?"

"Baby, it's probably a coincidence."

Baby....

Bull Schaffner told himself to buck up, to get a handle. They were idling again, stopped in the middle of the bend. "There's never just one cockroach, woman."

"I am a girl. A very special girl."

"Right. Now what? I can't turn around here."

"We don't need to turn around. That heifer lives across the road from the other roaches. We're almost there."

Bull eased the rig forward up a small hill, and as they neared the top the ditches on either side petered out. At the crest, on both sides, were large clearings with junk-filled yards interspersed with abandoned, forlorn-looking automobiles and fading house trailers. The old pickup was parked up against one of the trailers but the kids and the mopeds were nowhere in sight. Bull saw enough space to pull off the road and the truck hissed to a stop. He left the engine and the AC on.

"Showtime," Monkey said, and she popped out.

Bull took a few more seconds and shoved his 9mm Walther P-38 into the waist-band of his jeans, just above the .22 in the front pocket, pulled out his shirt to cover the pistols, and clipped on his cell phone. By the time he made it around the front of the tractor, Monkey was already pounding on doors. Children of various ages and dishabille began appearing — school was out for the summer — and one of the kids was jerked back inside by a woman in a flowery bikini. Bull's mouth dropped as Monkey dashed over to her trailer door and had a foot in it before it could be shut. No AC, a fan twirling listlessly in an open window with another of the new motorbikes leaning against it. Monkey said, "Where you getting all these new bikes?" The bikini woman was pulling on her front door with both hands and yelling: "Monkey, quit! Quit it, Monkey!"

Monkey jerked the door away from her, grabbed the lady's arm, and sent her sprawling down the trailer steps and onto the ground. "Where's my Danny? Where's his truck?"

Bull ambled up. It was a tony, thirtyish, dark-eyed, bottle-blonde lying there, wiping the dirt off her mouth with a hand. Bull avoided true blondes like the plague. So mercenary, so stuck on themselves, so competitive during divorce proceedings, so ..." He offered the downed woman a hand but Monkey slapped it away.

He unclipped his cell. "Call the law?"

"Oh, please, no," the lady said, making no attempt to get up. She adjusted her top, her eyes on Monkey.

"Get real, Bull," Monkey said. A circle of kids had formed around them now but not a one of them looked surprised or concerned. One of them was the overweight teenager, her arm with a smear of iodine swabbed over the place where it had been skinned by her moped accident.

"My daddy says we don't want no trouble. He says to show you where."

Monkey looked at her and sniffed. "Go inside and bring a towel. Tell him we'll bring you back."

"A towel?"

"The biggest one you got. A clean one!"

§

The dirt road was narrowing but Monkey assured Bull they would be hitting a blacktop highway soon. She was crouching between them, the big girl on the towel on the passenger seat.

Bull said, "I grew up near here but I never been on this one. Well, I was born in Miami but my folks moved here when I was ten or so."

"I seen Miami on TV," the girl said.

"You smell bad," Monkey said. "You ever take a bath?"

"I ain't had a chanst today yet. There! There's the road. Turn leff on it."

Bull geared down, and recognized the little highway immediately. "The pits road!" he said. And then he knew where Danny had been parking his rig.

The abandoned clay pits, deep and filled with water, were popular with adults and teenagers alike — swimming, tanning, barbecuing — and every summer featured a drowning or two. A trail behind them led to a weed-infested staging area where local truckers sometimes parked their rigs when they had a day or two off. The drivers themselves were not above lying prone atop the cliffs with binoculars to scope out the bikinis, and Bull had to smile when he realized that his own binoculars were within reach hanging behind his seat. Five minutes later he was easing around the largest of the pits in 3nd gear, the sun blazing down on the few parked cars and bathers, the big girl, Missy, saying, "Keep going, keep going" and Bull repeating, "No mopeds, nobody here with a moped."

"We didn' tell nobody."

On the other side of the pit Bull turned onto the trail he knew, bushes and low tree limbs scraping the sides of the tractor. In the next clearing, nothing, just empty space.

"Keep going," Missy said.

Bull stopped and pulled the air-brakes. "Here I can turn around. Can I down there?"

"No," Missy said. "We can walk from here." But she didn't move from her seat.

Impatient, Monkey clambered over Bull, steering wheel and all, slowing just enough to let her tube-top slide along his cheek. Sucking in a deep breath, he took the time to jam the 9mm Walther back into his waistband before following her down.

Monkey jerked open the other door. "Missy, out!"

"You're not the boss! It's far and it's hot!"

"You ever see the county jail? You want me to tell you what they do to a fully-loaded girl like you in there?"

"Like you would know."

"Oh, I certainly do know!" Monkey gave the big girl's leg a pull and Missy came tumbling out.

The three of them headed toward the next trail at the other end of the clearing, the women barefoot. Bull could feel the heat from the packed ground and wondered how they did it. Monkey, so full of energy, was leading, but stopped when she came to a fork.

Was she a jailbird, too? "Grass is all mashed on the left," Bull said.

Missy said, "The lef' one."

Bull caught up to Monkey but knew in his heart he would never be able to get close enough. Nevertheless he began to picture it, his head swimming with a hundred movies of how that would be, and suddenly they were up to another clearing and Monkey hollered.

"That's it!"

All Bull could see was a lone, baby-blue Ford pickup 250, clean and fairly new.

"That's my landlord's truck!" Monkey ran up to it, and Missy sat down on the dirt in a shady spot. In a second Monkey was poking around in the glove box and under the seat. "His gun's gone," she said matter-of-factly. A quick feel above the sun visors and she came up with a fat, folded stack of bills. With Bull right there, she sucked in her tummy and shoved the wad down into a front pocket of her tight shorts. The up-close sight of her toned abs and deep navel nearly short-circuited Bull's brain.

"Serve's him right," she explained.

"What?"

"I'm worth a lot more than what my rent is a month, that's what!"

Bull looked around again, and felt for the 9mm under his shirt, making sure it was still a quick draw. Missy was poking around in the dirt with a stick, not paying attention to anything. She looked up and said," That pickup's been here a week."

"You take his gun?"

"What gun?"

"Duh. Did you look?"

"I don' mess with no guns."

"Get up. Where's the big truck?"

Off in the distance from where they had come, Bull could hear the faint screams and hollers of kids goofing around in the water, and fragments of a boom-box playing some twangy, whiney country-western song. He was glad he had thought to shut down his rig so that the idling diesel would not block out any sounds, or attract attention.

"Up ahead," Missy grumped, and the three of them set off down a trail through the brush to the next clearing. This one had a small, muddy pit on one side and on the other, facing them, was Danny's truck. Bull could see that it hadn't rained since it was parked here, and it looked like the man knew the spot and had rutted a circle around the pit to turn around. Monkey was over there in a flash.

Bull turned to Missy. "I thought you said I couldn't turn around in here."

"Not with him in the way."

"Oh. Right. Duh."

Monkey came jouncing back. "Danny's bicycle is gone. The tractor's locked. The trailer doors are part open but the padlock isn't busted."

Bull swallowed. "Will you marry me?"

"There's a bicycle layin' in the bushes," Missy said, pointing.

"Oh Danny, Danny, Danny..." Monkey had the tip of her braid in her mouth and was chewing on it. "Okay, Bull, mister P.I., can you open Danny's cab?"

His pick set was back in his own truck, but chances were there was something in Danny's outboard toolbox, if that wasn't locked. Five minutes later Monkey was rummaging around inside the cab and came out with: "Danny's gun is gone, too!"

§

The big teenager, Missy, plunked down in the dirt again but this time it was Bull hauled her to her feet. "How many did you take?

"Um, five."

"Don't lie to me. This manifest says there should be thirty-two units."

"I ain't lyin'. The first time we got one, then we come back twicet and got two. I can count."

"Good. You can get up in there and help me count what's left."

"It's hot in there!"

Bull was hooking open the double doors. The pallets of one-gallon cans underneath the motor-bikes looked untouched, but the bikes themselves were stacked in such a way it would take some concentration to count. Not crated, but with quilted pads between each one. "You know how much a gallon of epoxy resin is worth?"

"Epoxy?"

Bull gave Missy a shove. "Get up in there!" He was wiping the palm of his hand on his jeans when Monkey came bounding up.

"I found a couple shell casings," she said. "Come on! Missy, get down from there!"

Bull said, "I'm the boss here!"

"Soon as we find Danny," Monkey said, and she was off.

The two shell casings were shiny, .45 ACPs. Bull picked one up. "Danny's gun an automatic?"

".45 Colt revolver. My landlord's is one of those army autos."

"Look. They were running. See? Boots digging in, long strides..."

"Another shell!"

It was another, stubby, .45 auto shell, lying a little off to the side of the trail Bull had spotted, gleaming brass in the sun still high above the trees. One set of boot prints sported deep lugs, with both sets of tracks heading close to the muddy pond and in the tire ruts Danny had made turning his rig around. Monkey dashed off, but half-way around the pond she stopped, her bare feet skidding on the loose dirt. Bending over to look, she suddenly bolted into the woods on that side.

Bull called after her to slow down, but with little enthusiasm. He followed more carefully, noting that even though she was running, her bare feet imprinted completely — small, square feet, (he pictured the red toenails) — and his heart pounded with desire. No, it was love. No, well, love and desire. "A ten-quote trip this is going to be," he said aloud. The clipboard was still in hand, and he hunted a safe place to set it down before following Monkey into the woods.

It looked bright up ahead finally, another clearing coming up, and Bull stopped to pick up another shell casing. Monkey had missed it: another .45 auto. Bull stopped and listened. If Danny took his own gun before running off, and it was a .45 Colt revolver, a single hit from that 250-grain slug would knock a man down, and the longer .45 caliber shell casing would still be in the gun. If it didn't kill the man there would be serious bleeding. He looked around. It was quiet here, and peaceful, and apparently too far from the swimming hole to hear any partying. But there was a buzzing nearby. A beehive? Then he heard running. Monkey returned, breathing hard for the first time.

"I lost the trail."

"Shhhh...!"

"Flies!" Before Bull could react she was off toward the noise, and Bull followed her leaps through the thickets. He could smell it before he could catch up to her. Lying face up, the face eaten half away, was a putrid body, lug-soled boots pointing right at Bull, a cloud of metallic-green bottle-flies swarming over a torn open shirt and the blue-gray skin of a man's fat belly with a single, black bullet hole in it. A Model 1911 automatic lay beside the man's right hand, the hammer cocked for another shot. After a moment of hesitation, Bull and Monkey quietly circled the body, both of them looking way into the thicket from time-to-time for signs of Danny. Monkey finally stopped over the cocked handgun and bent down to pick it up.

"Hey!" Bull said. "This is a crime scene!"

Monkey halted, her right hand inches from the weapon. "This is a good gun!"

"Yeah, well, just please, this once, be a citizen?"

Monkey straightened up. "A citizen?" She began to laugh, then broke into tears. "Danny," she said.

"He can't be far from here." Bull put his arms around her and she hugged back, holding onto him for the longest time — too long to make any sense — her glossy, sleek head under his chin and her high-strung body clinging against his. Bull was forgetting why they were embracing, and just in time they were both startled by Missy's screaming. Monkey broke away and Bull followed her back the way they had come, all the way to the clearing with Danny's truck. Missy was kneeling beside the muddy pond and wailing.

"They's a body! It's dead! It's gross!"

The mud-covered length of a man was barely visible, sunken in the way it was, and they had walked right past it earlier when they were following the trail of boot prints. Now Bull could see they had also missed the lighter set of prints doubling back. Monkey plowed into the mud and began plunging her arms into and around the ooze. "It's Danny!"

"Crime scene! Get out of there!"

"Shut up, Bull! Missy, git!"

The big girl did not require any persuading, and was off and running. Bull hollered for her to stop but she kept on going and he was not able to catch up to her until she had made it half way back to his own rig. Much stronger than he had anticipated, she nearly nailed a direct knee jab to his groin but settled down after he managed to wrest an arm behind her back.

"I weren't goin' nowhere!" she yelled. "I was gonna wait here! I weren't goin' to call the law or nothin'!"

"Wait right here then!" Bull headed back to the pond on a run just in time to see Monkey sliding a wallet, surprisingly clean, out of Danny's back pocket. She had dragged him half way up onto dry ground, and was kneeling beside him. She fished out a small wad of bills, slid the wallet back into the pocket, and stood up. Dripping.

"I put it back so they can identify him," she said. "Crime scene." She did not look very upset about it. "Looks like he was shot a couple times and maybe he tried running back to his truck and fell in here."

"I love it when you suck in your tummy," Bull said. "You are so beautiful."

"Thank you." The money stashed, Monkey faced Bull for a moment.

Splattered with mud, Monkey was attracting flies herself, and even so Bull could not remember ever being so besotted with a woman as he was now. He watched her turn and slog back into the mud, her arms plunging up-and-down where Danny's body had lain.

Bull came to his senses. "Get out of there!"

"I can beat your ass!"

"What are you doing!? This is a crime scene. They'll find traces of you on the body and stuff."

"In this county? That's just on TV, Bull. There's probably not a cop for twenty miles! Leave me alone! Danny's gun is down here somewhere! It's a real Colt .45!"

"I'll buy you another one! Get out of there!"

Monkey stood and faced him, and Bull suddenly flashed on one of his father's fantasies: Moonbeam McSwine from the "Lil Abner" comic strip.

"Come out of there, Moonbeam. Come on."

Monkey's lips parted, and she suddenly smiled. She knew.

Bull reached her a hand. "Come on. We have business to take care of."

§

The lady in the big house came to the door without the baseball bat this time, and Bull described the abandoned pickup truck. It was getting dark now, and the porch light was on. Monkey was right behind him, nodding her head at the details.

"Yup, that sounds like Billy's. Your bobble-head here would know."

"Billy kinda fat? Big belly?"

"Yep. Why?"

"He's been shot."

The lady hesitated, but only for a split second. "Dead?"

"Killed dead," Monkey said. "For days now, smells like."

"Shut up, little hussy girl." The woman's mouth suddenly opened, and then she smiled. "You better be telling the truth!"

"Dead," Bull said.

"Ohhhh!" She came down the two steps and gave Bull a startling, enthusiastic hug. "You're not messing with me now, are you?"

Monkey said, "No, Ma'am. He's killed dead."

"Ohhhh!" The lady broke away from Bull and reached for Monkey, pulling her close. She gave Monkey a big, noisy kiss on top of her head. Back to Bull, she nearly nailed him with a kiss on the lips. He backed away.

"Life insurance?"

"You better believe it! I make sure the payments are up-to-date myself! Ohhhh!"

"Good." Bull caught her eye with his *stern* look. "We have some details to work out before we call the law. I'm a P.I., remember?"

"Oh, yeah, right, sure, ha ha, private, okay okay! Ohhhh!" She plunked down on the porch steps and Bull sat down beside her.

Monkey, her legs in a wide stance, stood there, fists on hips. In the yellow bug-light she was a dream splattered with dried mud. "I'm hungry," she said. "I haven't eaten all day!"

"I have some steaks thawed out," the lady said. "There's a grill out back. Mushroom and grilled onion gravy. New potatoes all ready to scrub in the sink. Mister, you light the grill and little hussy here can scrub the potatoes and I'll get a frying pan with some olive oil going, and, oh, I'm sorry, my name's Evita."

"Evita...." Bull got to his feet. "I knew it! A ten-quote trip for sure."

"Monkey said, "What?"

"I'll explain that later."

"You can explain that now!"

"Yes, now," Evita said. She was twirling her short, side-loader braids and looking quite pleased with herself.

All three in the kitchen now, large and clean, with the back yard looking festive through the windows, the patio area lit up with yellow bug-lights. Bull was sitting on a stool watching the two women, each a different brand of weird. He wished Monkey were sitting on his lap. "My company wants me to take Danny's rig and load to Houston so they can get paid, then haul back here where they'll send another driver down and I can pick up my own truck, which means I need to get Danny's out of the clay pits like now."

"You phoned your company? They told you that? Yeah, right."

"It's a small company. Family company. The five motorbikes the kids stole they can write off, and the kids, or Missy, can call the law tomorrow morning and act like they discovered the bodies by accident. That way the investigation won't impound Danny's truck, which would cost everybody way too much money."

Evita was shaking her head over the frying onions and bell peppers. "Those retards up on Morton's Hill are your robots now? I don't think so."

"I told Missy I'd ship her to Mogadishu in a live-animal cage if she didn't do as told."

"I'm coming along," Monkey said.

"No, you're staying here and making sure Missy..."

"Why call the law at all?!"

"So wives can collect insurance, for one thing."

"Oh. Okay, but I'm still coming along. It's my boyfriend's truck."

"Was your boyfriend's truck."

"Time to turn the steaks, Bull," Evita said.

Evita also had mosquito lanterns burning out there, the kind that worked: candle inside with a repellant tab on top you replaced every four hours. Bull moved the steaks up onto the top rack, turned the propane down a little, and closed the lid. God, how he loved the smell of burning meat! He was hungry, also, and they'd all be chowing down soon. His high spirits, however, were coming from the amazing combination of exciting things which were happening, and their all coming together at one time was more than he could handle.

Back inside, he nearly shouted it. "I need a drink!"

Evita smiled. She was talking to somebody on the phone and kept on talking while she pulled out an almost-full liter of Jack Daniel's from behind the microwave. "What I'm saying is," Evita said, "if you come over now and pull those posts out like immediately, you can have them all. That's the deal. Now. I have a family truck-driver friend here needs to park off the road tonight."

An hour later, Evita and Bull and Monkey were three sheets to the wind.

§

Midnight. stars. Half moon. No swimmers or lovers around the main pit, and Evita, driving her unpretentious, dark-blue Corsica, dropped Bull and Monkey off after turning around at Billy's pickup. They had decided to leave Billy's vehicle alone, but Bull had Monkey wipe off whatever fingerprints she may have left looking for his gun earlier. Monkey seemed pretty steady on her feet, but Bull worried about himself. On the way out he'd have to ease Danny's big rig around and there was barely enough room, well, Evita had given them an extra set of keys in case they needed to move the pickup a little.

Bull said, "Evita! Don't get a D.U.I. on the way back!"

"Like there's cops on duty around here? Ha ha. Not in this county. You can't even get anybody dialing 9-1-1 around here!"

By the time they had Danny's truck back at the crossroads, all the posts had been pulled out and two men were loading them into a small, dump truck. Bull parked Danny's rig up near the intersection at Monkey's place, and pulled his own unit off the highway in front of Evita's house. Evita was passed out on her living-room couch, so Monkey got right to cleaning up Danny's tractor while Bull brought over the few items he thought he would need from his own tractor for the Houston trip. "Mine has an extra bunk on top," he said, surprised at his nervousness. He hoped Monkey had not detected his sudden unease.

"Get real, Bull."

"Uhhh...."

"You know you're dying to get in the sack with me."

"I, oh, jeez, Monkey, I, uh..."

"Can you put that into words?"

"Seems you dropped Danny from your life without a whimper."

"You think I'm dumb, too, besides all my good stuff? And heartless? I have a heart with a brain. Danny was using me."

"And you're not using me?"

"We're using each other, and I am not dumb. We need to get it on right here in the truck, tonight, now, before we do anything else, and before we leave, and then maybe you can relax and you can walk and talk at the same time again."

§

At the rest area off I-10 east of Pensacola, they pulled off to park briefly so they could do it again. Monkey said she needed to use the bathroom first and while she was gone Bull talked to a local on a motorcycle who was selling jewelry. "This here's a real ruby," the man said, and although the sky was overcast the gem did have a remarkable brilliance to it. It was a faceted, red sphere about the size of a large pea, and Bull got him down from fifty bucks to twenty. When Monkey returned he gave it to her, and she squealed with delight, jumping up and down on the tarmac. An hour later, the two of them sat in silence for a few minutes while Monkey looked at Bull's interstate trucking map and Bull explained what to expect on the trip. She said, "We can't stop in New Orleans? I never been there."

"Not this time, but..."

"Oh, I'm so happy about this ruby!" She held it up to the windshield and rolled it around between her fingers."

"It might not be real."

"I can see it's real!" She leaned over and kissed his ear. "I love it! Nobody ever gives me a present!"

Bull found that hard to believe, plus her closure regarding Danny was too quick and easy. Her delight seemed genuine, though, and Bull remembered that this was one of the items on his father's list. "Yup, Bull said. "A ten-quote trip this is for sure!"

"Okay, that's it. We don't leave here 'til you explain that."

Bull smiled, and reached for the small, leather-covered, loose-leaf binder on the dashboard. He was glad he had remembered to bring it. It was his favorite accessory. "My dad gave me this old notebook a couple years ago, the one where he wrote quotes from famous people over the years. Dad says that everything in life has already happened before, and people smarter than us wrote it all down. He used to tell me that everything that will ever happen to me is in here." Bull flipped through the worn pages, some written in pencil but most in blue or black ink. He by-passed the Morton's Fork entry, which he knew by heart and had been written early and near the beginning, written maybe when his father was younger than his own age, barely legible in light pencil, a long paragraph. He spotted the Moonbeam McSwine quote and passed that up, too, until he found what he was looking for. Bull said, "I should call you Sacagawea. That young, Indian girl who was the translator-guide on the Lewis and Clark expedition. She ..."

Monkey said, "Something I did?"

"Yup."

"So what's it say?"

Bull squinted his eyes and read aloud. "Captain Meriwether Lewis: If Sacagawea has enough to eat and a few trinkets to wear I believe she would be perfectly content anywhere."

An hour later Bull's heart was beginning to hurt with love. Chest pain and knives in his gut. They were roaring through the tunnel under the river at Mobile now, dark thoughts piercing Bull's euphoria, Monkey at the edge of her seat taking it all in. "They should wash these tiles," she said.

"You sure were rough on that woman in the bikini you threw in the dirt at the trailer park."

"It not a trailer park. It's like a tiny town. It's called the Morton Hill Community. That was my mother."

Silence....

Bull decided not to pursue that. The truth no longer mattered. Going down the road with a tiger in the bunk looked like a kitten, what more could a driver ask for? Nevertheless he couldn't stop wondering. "Community? Sounds religious."

Monkey did not respond.

"Monkey, what religion are you?"

She answered immediately. "I'm a Frisbeetarian. I believe that when you die your soul flies up on the roof and stays there."

§

Bull watched her run through the rain between the fuel-pumps to the small convenience store to score a six-pack of beer. They were just outside Baton Rouge, and despite being giddy with new love, Bull's dilemma was beginning to nag at him. If Monkey stayed with him for any length of time at all, he would never see his children again. He would lose his 40 acre paradise in West Virginia, and... (He blocked out all the other stuff.) If Monkey left him he would be heartbroken, and something like her was a once-in-a-lifetime deal. But he was also beginning to see that his dilemma was going to solve itself. It was looking like Monkey had never really been anywhere large before, and this trip was her fantasy. All of North America lay ahead. Bull knew what the most likely stops would be when he was back in his own rig. Atlanta, Chicago, Montreal, Boston, New York City, D.C., Miami, and somewhere along the way she would realize he was too old for her and Monkey would jump ship. *Or....* Bull shut his eyes and rubbed his head. Monkey had admitted she worked off her rent sometimes. Now she needed to find storage for her stuff. He pictured her disappearing into the rental office for nearly an hour, and coming out with a key and a number and a smile. This unreal girl would eventually evaporate leaving memories too fantastic to share because they would be too unbelievable or too hard to bear. "Typical truck driver story" other drivers would say. And then Bull would maybe go fishing for a couple days, and cry in his beer, and then call dispatch to see where he was headed next, and decide which would be closest to his route. Miami, or Milwaukee, or his 40 acres up in the West Virginia hills where his two boys would maybe remember their father, maybe not, and their mother might or might not be happy to see him. •

JOHN AALBORG

Read more of Bull Schaffner's adventures, illegal wives, neglected children, and vigilante justice with a heart — in the crime novel "LOWBOY #22"

Giorgio Possum

Howard squinted at the numbers tacked to the wall beside the kitchen phone. The pharmacy was all the way in town so he stooped over the table to jot down a list. Garden gloves, disposable razors, his prescriptions.... Maybe he could pay the insurance late this one time and mail Beverly the Giorgio. She used to linger at the perfume counter, and when he would hurry her along she would mention Julie, a sewing factory co-worker. Someone had given Julie a small bottle of Giorgio — so expensive.

Julie had been Howard's girlfriend before he met Beverly at the girls' company party.

After Beverly married him but long before their divorce, Howard found an abandoned, newborn opossum — tiny, pink, and helpless. Beverly eagerly took it under her wing and named him George — later, Giorgio. Since Beverly was so young and could be neglectful of him at times, Howard marveled at her caring and love for Giorgio.

On hold after dialing the pharmacy, Howard gazed at the photo on the wall: the fully-grown and plump, furry possum in Beverly's arms — as big now as a puppy — Giorgio's thumb and slender fingers curling around her long braid. Howard had insisted on an outdoor pen and Beverly would go there first, after work, to get him out for a hug. Giorgio lived almost three years, and his grave was near the front door of the trailer. On his way to the car, Howard bent over the marker he had made and brushed away a tear from his cheek, and the dead leaves and ground-litter from Giorgio's name and dates.   •

Passion's Perch

Tricia

I'm fourteen now. No dates, no bad habits, and no pimples. My parents, however, blossom in all three categories. You might say I'm living proof that blighted genes and a messed-up environment can still produce a good kid. How good? Let me disgust you.

Dad finally brought home an interesting date. Too interesting, especially for my brother. David is two years older than me, and he's very smart. Smart about school stuff, anyway: straight A's, hardly ever does any homework, reads a book and remembers everything.... Actually, I test almost as high as he does every year, but I carry my smarts over into real life. David boogers through every day like a Neanderthal. Mom says it's because he's a boy. Hey, did Billy-Jeff Clinton, when he was a boy, flick his tongue at girls with ocean-depth cleavage, and roll out a burp just because he was a male? Well.... Okay, forget I said that.

At first I didn't think much about it — my brother and Dad's date. I have my own life. And with Mom gone, maybe for good, I don't have the time to be David's psychiatrist. But lately I've begun to worry. I'll be going on real dates myself soon, and I think about that a lot. I picture how I'm going to do everything, especially how I'm going to escape from stuff that gets too heavy, or how it will all feel if I don't. I've even practiced with the handle of the bathroom potty-plunger on how to roll the condom over his thing. (Dad calls condoms "balloons"). This girl in school, Lunette Curry, she says they like you to do it for them, roll it on for them. So while I'm practicing it I say stuff to reassure the plunger-stick that without it he ain't gettin' none — in this low, sultry, firm-as-nails but sexy voice — when nobody's home, of course!

Then I think about how dearmost brother David acts and I listen to his opinions on what girls are for and it gets scary. See, Dad lets David go out at night without our knowing where he's headed or when he'll be back. But when it comes to me, I can be taking the garbage bag out after supper and Dad'll ask me where I'm going! So even though I know I'm the younger one, nobody can tell me that I'm not trotting around in chains because I'm a female.

Anyway, Dad got custody of both of us during the divorce last year, but we talk to Mom a lot on the phone. The deal was she wasn't supposed to see us in person until she went through this long, detox program (she lasted three days). And even though she seems to be trying to cure herself, Dad still takes a firm attitude about visitation. So we don't get contaminated and addicted — as if we would. But when Dad's job takes him away from home for more than a day he gets all mellowed out about Mom and they make these little deals, which we have to keep secret. Then she babysits with us, here, overnight. Well, that's all over with now that it's rutting season.

The new heifer's name is Marcella.

David

At first, Tricia pretended to be unimpressed with the latest achievement of Dad's mating skills. Tricia is a "lady" now — so she claims — and she believes that this new definition of herself enhances our family reality since Mom split. (Trish's boring fourteenth birthday was only last month). But to me the only lady with any class I've seen here lately is this leggy, star-quality boozer Dad managed to snag.

Trish's understanding of the word lady doesn't include high-born, or elegant, or classy — the qualities of ladies of history. Ladies of today drive tractor-trailer trucks. They go fishing and bait their own hooks. They trade colors and flavors of unopened condom packs in school, and flop for skin-heads and drop-outs. (I have a genius IQ and am probably the only male virgin left in my homeroom). These modern ladies have other, even higher priorities, of course. A lady smokes and has to hold her cigarette just right, and blow the smoke in her date's face. I digress....

The reason I mention Tricia baiting her own fish hook is because the day we were so rudely awakened to the seriousness of Dad's dating requirements, Tricia and I were planning a "quality time" fishing trip with him. And Lady Tricia sure can jam a helpless wiggle-worm onto a hook without a thought! Besides indifference to routine cruelties, young ladies are also prone to use echo-speech. A man never uses redundancies like wiggle-worm, or roach-bug, or crawly-bug, or un-safe sex. But Tricia is smart in her own way — she can always get Dad to take us fishing, even when he doesn't want to. I can be sitting there at the supper table telling him the whole, beautiful, weekend weather report, how it's going to be perfect, through Monday, and Dad'll be glomming out the window at the backyard — missing Mom again probably — mumbling about how the boat motor didn't seem to be running right last time (it hauled like Orca) and how great it would be to sleep late for a change on Saturday. All Tricia has to do, however, is say: "Oh, please, Daddy?"

OK, I'm with Trish in the living-room getting tackle ready. There are parents who'd kill to have two trustworthy teenagers behave like this when they're late coming home from work on Friday. I hear the car pull up. I'm thinking: We've got him! He can't turn us down when he sees what we're doing! And Trish isn't racing out the back door to meet him, either — something Dad really hates. "Give me five minutes!" he's always saying. "Just five minutes!" But he usually ends up swooping Tricia up off her feet anyway for the big, warm hug that I don't seem to rate anymore.

Trish is busy putting the fish-hooks back into the little compartments in the box according to size, like she's suddenly not into running out to hug Dad before he can even get his briefcase out of the trunk. I'm just about to inquire, you know, toss her a cut, and she says: "It's not our car, David."

I listen. The motor is still running. It has a deep, rumbling sound — not at all like the sewing-machine motor in the Kia Dad bought after Mom left. I hear an American car-door slam.

"Give them five minutes," Tricia says sweetly.

I shoot Trish a bird and head for the window — and groan with genuine pain. Lady Tricia is right next to me and trying to mash me to the side with her elbow so she can get a better look. I mumble my thoughts: "Look what Dad lured here. Foxier than Mom.... Too hard to see from here but it's still going to be the same routine.... Maybe...."

"Not foxier, David," Trish grumps. "She wasn't lured here. You need to get out of the animal kingdom!"

"Kingdom?" I love to nail her on PC correctness crap.

The woman is trying to reach through the window of her old Camaro for the inevitable bag of groceries. Duhhh.... Like, whatever happened to getting out the bag and then closing the door? Trish and I both let out a simultaneous moan. The grocery bag has long, leafy green stuff poking out at the top.

"Creepy veggies," Trish sighs.

"Our reward for being good." We hear the back door open and Dad saying: "Wait till you meet the kids!"

Trish stomps her foot — definitely princess material. We head for the kitchen. Other single parents go out on dates! Dad is reaching for the woman's hand, like to lead her in, even though she's got both arms around the groceries. A real gentleman. He sounds funny, too. It's his dating voice.

"The kids, uhhhh, do the dishes every day after school, but..."

"You said you'd take us to Burger King today!" Trish says, ignoring our failure.

"And we were getting the tackle ready!" I chime in.

Anger is blooming on Dad's face.

"We forgot the dishes, Daddy!" Trish rushes up to him and scores her big hug. I look at the date, fine-tuning my original appraisal. The thing I'm noticing now, suddenly, is that she's not wearing a bra. Great! Just this short, tight little muscle-shirt with DAYTONA BEACH imprinted on the front. A little flat-chested but pointy, and her jeans are nicely molded on, plus she's trotting these high-clog, leather sandals. Definitely not the vitamin-C and prune-juice lane Dad's been cruising lately. I reach out and accept the bag with the green stuff peeking out, and nearly drop it because of the unexpected weight. The coldness of the bag at the bottom and the clink of bottles reminds me of Mom coming home from the store. "Corona? Heineken?" I scale down the enthusiasm. "Miller? Budweiser?"

"Don't be a smart-ass, Son." Dad's doing his best to control his wrath regarding the messy dishes overflowing both sides of the kitchen sink. "Marcy? Meet my two young'uns! David and Tricia!"

DAVID & TRICIA! LIVE!

I extend my free hand like a true member of the male elite, realizing, but just for a second, that this whole bit could be fun. Dad's date was as tall as me. She flashed her pearly-whites and clasped my hand in both of hers.

"And I'm Tricia," I hear my sister saying through the excitement, as if who-was-who would be a problem. The creature then takes Tricia's head in both hands like she was a precious vase or something, and begins stroking Trish's eyebrows with her thumbs. For another evanescent twinkling of clarity I know that we are in the presence of a superior force. Dad, obviously nervous, grabs the bag and whacks the bottles out of the six-pack carton, lining them up in the fridge. He's lining them up in there in a perfect row just like Mom used to, only when she would do it Dad would say: "The refrigerator's not church, Honey. It's just a machine to keep things cold." And then I catch Trish's eye and we both nod. Knowledge. This would be a big one. I sneak another, hard look at Dad's catch.

Definitely foxy. And nice little hooters, you know, up there. No problem with the laws of physics like gravity. But not Dad's type — at least I wouldn't think so. Like when they show previews of what's coming on the next re-runs of "Soul Train", I know for a fact that Dad tenses up when the dancers bounce their stuff. One night, when we were allowed to stay up late for some reason and a re-run of an old "Soul Train" was about to come on, Trish grabbed the remote control, not to be a bitch but just to see what was on the other channels for a second. Dad reached out and snatched the remote away and held Trish back with his arm, his fingers all splayed out like he was playing guard in basketball, his eyeballs riveted to the tube. But, hey! What are fathers for if not to re-enforce a son's education? You're right, Dad. "Soul Train" dancers are pure, gender-specific, hooter-pots from Hell! Or they used to be at some ancient time.

"David!" Dad's voice pierces my horny reverie. "Get up this tackle! It's all over the living-room!"

"Coming!" I toss a manly wink at the lady-friend and exit the kitchen looking for Trish, who has conveniently disappeared. I turn around and glance back into the kitchen, remembering how hungry I am. The new person is fondling the dark-green, fluffy-looking stuff with the crinkly leaves — certainly not the fuel I was designed for. I look Marcy over once more and get caught before I get back to her face. My gaze furtively meets her eyes. Lids painted dark blue.

Musky eye shadow with sparkly stuff in it extending way past the outside corners, like Cleopatra. Her fingers loaded with rings....

"I'm looking for the cutting board," she says sweetly.

"It pulls out." I show her. I notice the little lines at the corners of her mouth. Around her eyes, too. But she's sure a lot younger than Mom. Dad is yelling again and I boogie for the living-room. I'm preparing myself for the inevitable cancellation of the fishing trip we had planned for the next morning.

Dad suddenly swings to a better mood. Well, sure, he's in heat! Anyway, he had most of the stuff already put away. "Don't worry, Davey. We're still going. I invited Marcy to come along."

"And she said yes?!"

Dad gives me his long, cold look — then smiles. "She couldn't resist."

"Yeah, well, how did you do it? I mean, how did you meet her?" It was a good time to get back on Dad's good side.

"She's an E.M.T. — and ambulance driver — at the county hospital. On my route."

Dad's a salesman for medical equipment. He's always telling us gross, super gory hospital stories at supper time. But he never mentioned any girl ambulance jockey.

"She just got her certificate to teach EVOC, too! Emergency vehicle operation. She can drive, Son. She sure can drive!" Dad is waiting for some sign of my approval of this heady information, while I poker-face it and picture Marcy hauling ass through town with all the sirens and the lights blazing. Dad tries again. "And she's not bad looking, either!"

Man-to-man stuff. I manage an inscrutable smile.

He winks. "Well, show Marcy where everything is. I've got to get a shower!"

Thank you, Tricia, for disappearing. I am now alone in the kitchen with this new hot-rod version of Mom busting eggs open with one hand while clutching a Busch-Light in the other. I move up to observe how she does it. She makes it look so easy. crack plop whup The empty shells are whacking into the garbage thing while one of her sexy, sandal-shod feet is stepping on the little pedal that holds the lid open. Her toenails are bright red but a lot of the paint is chipped off like Mom's always seemed to be. I can't help looking Marcy up-and-down again. Hey, I didn't invent my male instincts! Maybe its the fact she's an EMT and ambulance driver that is stoking the attraction. Yeah, and I'm feeling this tugging in my chest. My heart. The other ladies Dad brought home were so blah. You could lose track of them the way they blended into the wall paper.

"I'm strictly a meat and potatoes and gravy man," I blurt out. "My mother spoiled me, I guess."

"That's okay," she shoots back, popping the last egg. "How old are you."

"Fifteen." I successfully suppressed the going-on-sixteen bit.

"Well. Your Dad tells me you're smart for your age. Fifteen, huh? I have a little girl, well, she's not little anymore.... She's thirteen now but looks a lot older. A lot older. She's, well...."

I move back and pull out a chair from the table. I'm waiting for her to finish, but she seems consumed by the desire to chop into smithereens the weird, green stuff. The same vegetable matter, I realize, she is planning to crucify the eggs with.

"Thirteen?" I was counting back and she turned and saw my lips moving. "You don't look..." I stop. I'm picturing Dad around the corner, maybe listening in.

"I had Pashy when I was very, very young."

"Pashy?"

She stopped chopping and was looking me smack in the eye, the knife poised in mid-air. She starts to smile. "We were crazy back then, my ex and me, and we named her Passion."

I'm thinking: how did they know what she would be like when she grew up, like what if she grew up to be dorky and ugly, with a name like Passion.

"Before your gears get jammed, we wanted her to be hot stuff when she matured." Marcy turns back to the cutting board. "We were thinking of her, not how we got her."

I hadn't even thought about that!

From my low, sitting position I try to cop a peek under that short muscle-shirt and am rewarded, instead, with a painfully brief but clear view through an arm hole — of a nipple! I know, I know, there are more important things in this life — I just don't know what they are yet. The meaningful stuff can triumph later.

Dad suddenly returns from his shower. Resplendent. White shorts. White sneakers with his favorite pair of socks, the ones with "NIKE" woven into the cuffs. His black JACK DANIEL'S T-shirt.

"How's it going, guys?" His I'm happy — I'm cool act.

"Dad! Your Captain Midnight shirt! I thought that was reserved for..."

His heavy, iron grip clamped onto my shoulder and began to mash the ten-billion or so cells there. Real pain. Intense, Biblical pain, and Dad's Friday-evening score is backing him up.

"We all are looking for happiness, David. Each in his own way."

"See, Son?" Dad's grip tightens one more notch just in time to prevent me from being able to say: That's what you said the last time!

Instead, I blurt like a lamb. "I was explaining to, uh...."

"Marcy," they both say.

"I was explaining the, uh, meat and potatoes and..."

"Gravy," Dad says.

"Same goes for me!" Trish waltzes into the kitchen wearing her terry-cloth, Day-Glo playsuit which Dad had made her promise to throw away because it displayed a blinding flash of her butt cheeks. I make a note to myself that in addition to the cheek show, the top half of her outfit would be filled out better than Marcy's in another month or so.

"My sister thinks she has to prove she's blossoming out," I hear myself say. But Dad is slowly releasing his grip on my shoulder as this new reality sinks in.

"Pashy's growing, too!" Marcy says brightly. She slips me a wink. "You might even like it!" She pauses. "I mean, her."

"Gotchya the first time!"

We both laugh. I watch the chopped foliage get dumped into the eggs.

"Frying pan," Marcy says.

My forehead and Dad's collide at the bottom cupboard where the pots and pans are stashed. Like I said, a superior force. I defer to my father and back away so he can proffer the desirable female the frying pan. Marcy, in the meantime, had whisked a cold one out of the fridge along with the bacon package in a single, deft stroke. Another memory reared its ugly head. Those twist-off caps on beer bottles — when Mom was having too many she could slip one of those caps off without a sound. It was so sneaky. Mr. Harris, our next-door neighbor, drinks beer out of cans and when he's out on his front porch getting bombed you can hear the *pschttt!* when he boldly rips the tab off the next one. Anyway, I've promised myself never to let stuff like beer get a hold on me. I'm going to be independent. What if a war starts one day? There's fifty of them going on in the world right now — what if one starts here? Where are people like Mom going to get their alcohol, their cigarettes, their drugs? Huh? But people like me, all we will have to score every day is food.

I used to hang out at this one kid's house — his parents were always nice to me but they both smoked cigarettes and drank beer and smoked grass. I was over there one night when they were out of pot and they had this big discussion about who they knew who would have some reefer and how much it would cost, et cetera. It was pitiful, you know, because they were already too zonked to do anything about it and they eventually let the whole thing go. I was also over there on another night when it was storming — it was getting late and I was hoping they would eventually offer me a ride home — when a big commotion fired up in the kitchen about who drank the last beer. The argument was over in seconds. Suddenly we were all heading for their car and getting soaking wet in the downpour. The addicts scored their beer first, the legal stuff, then dropped me off at home. On the night they were out of pot but had plenty of beer, I had to walk.

I feel Dad's hand on my shoulder again, gentle this time. "You okay, Son?"

"He day-dreams," Tricia says in her *I-know-how-everything-is* voice. "Sometimes after school, before you come home, he'll be staring out the window, dreaming, and he'll start to twitch and stuff and then his foot kicks out and he has to quick catch himself so he won't fall out the chair."

"I thought I told you to get rid of that playsuit, young lady." Dad in his model-parent mode.

"Mommy gave it to me. We have a deal about stuff like that."

"But I also told you that..."

"A deal is a deal! At least it used to be!"

"She's so pretty!" Marcy chimes in.

I suck in another deep breath. I get straight A's in school, right? Always have. I sent the SSAT test computer off scale — top one percent in the nation! Tricia gets C's. Last time even a D — she's that lazy. But she's pretty. She's a chick. See what I mean? And they say it's a man's world.... Dad took us to see the movie "Amadeus" one time. Near the end, in the nut-house, Salieri was preaching to everyone that God was the Patron of Mediocrity. When the movie was over and we were riding home in the ingenuous Kia, Trish asked Dad what mediocrity meant. Dad slowed down without a word, and leaned over and gave Tricia a hug.

More and more I see myself as one of those people who will produce wonderful things, like

Wolfgang Amadeus Mozart, and not be recognized as a treasure-for-all-time until after death.

Suddenly, while I'm thinking all this great stuff, the sun peeks out. I mean, Marcy comes over to where I am sitting and hooks an arm around my head, pressing it against her in this wonderful hug. I'm instantly overwhelmed. My mind boggles and tries to deny any knowledge of which exact part of her body I am being loved against, but it's soft and firm at the same time and I can feel that nipple! It's her big hug, I'm sure. She understands!

But then she turns me loose, just as suddenly, and goes over to Tricia and lays a big one on her! With kisses! For the millionth time in my life I am forced to believe that gremlins stay glued to my channel, reading my mind and messing with it — playing hardball with my life.

Tricia proudly plunks down in the chair next to mine and leans back, looking down at her chest. Dad and Marcy don't see it.

"It'll be a toss-up soon," I say.

"Tune in next week." Trish chortles her evil, Bart Simpson laugh. We both quiet down to listen in on the new development gaining in volume. They're arguing already? In the middle of it, Marcy opens the fridge and has a new bottle out so quickly that nobody sees her twist the cap off. Her other hand is empty, as if the Busch she's holding is the same one she had before. "The Magic Beer Bottle Trick". Now both of them are into the fridge groping around for the cheese while Dad counts remaining bottles, pretending to be helping.

I want to help, too. "Only one left, Dad."

"We had fried cheese sandwiches last night, Pop," Trish reminds him. "We used it all, remember?"

"Yeech!" Marcy says. "This bread!" She had spotted the brand new loaf of our favorite, soft, white bread and is waving it in Dad's face. The loaf is kinking in the middle, mashing the premium slices. "This is junk food!"

"I'll go to the store," Dad says meekly, "and..."

"No, I'll go. I'm off!" Her long legs are already flashing toward the back door, the heels of her platform sandals clicking like firecrackers. Jeans and clogs, ahhhhh....

Half-way out the door she blows Dad a kiss.

Dad sighs and sits down at the table with us. We listen while Marcy's old Camaro fires up and burns rubber backwards out of the drive. Dad sighs again, but he's smiling. Like he does when he's eating ice-cream and there's more in the fridge. He looks back-and-forth between us for the favorable comments we might be giving this one.

From down the block comes the chirp when Marcy shifts into second.

"Well, she can drive, Dad." He looks at me, waiting for more. I give in. "She's different. And she's not boring. Definitely not charm-challenged."

"She reminds me of Mom a little," Trish says.

Just what I'd been thinking but didn't want to admit. "But younger. More — lively. Foxy."

Just the animal reference Dad was trolling for. His smile broadens.

After a long silence, Trish says, "Will she last till supper's done? You know, I mean, is she going to pass out — before?"

I was going to add that I hoped she wouldn't pass out before getting back from the store but I hold my tongue. She isn't that drunk yet, anyway, although if she's like Mom she has a backup whiskey bottle in the car. But Dad is looking sad now. He shrugs and gets up to survey the progress on our dinner.

"Well, nothing's burning!"

"You have to turn on the burners for that," Tricia says.

Cute, but it didn't amuse Dad, who is really looking pitiful now. Suddenly Trish blurts out: "I love you, Daddy!"

For the first time I don't hate her for saying trite stuff.

"I love you too, Dad."

We wait. Never has the kitchen been so quiet. It seems to be getting very warm, also, at least for me. "The oven is on!"

Dad starts to get out of his chair but eases back down. "It's on pre-heat."

Trish giggles. "We're having baked eggs?"

Another long silence. We're all thinking about Mom, I know it. Dad finally says, "You guys never did let me see her last letter. Has she called lately?"

"She said she misses us."

"She said she stopped drinking again."

"That's what she always says."

We were telling about the last phone call. Her letter Trish had tried to flush down the toilet along with a spent rag, a mess I had to fish out and then promise not to tell. Dad had put a special container in the bathroom for that kind of girl stuff....

"And she wanted to know if all three can fit in the Kia."

This time we all laugh.

"You didn't have to get the smallest Kia they make, Dad," Trish says.

"They build faster ones, too."

"Not as fast as Marcy's Camaro, I bet, dear brother."

I think about that for a minute and then hear the devil itself returning — the Camaro squealing off the avenue onto our street for the final approach. In seconds Marcy comes dazzling into the house with the cheese. No bag. That meant the new six-pack was still in the car. With one side of me telling me to forget it, I get up and tell everyone I have to go out and inspect the muscle-car. I explain. "It sounded so good when you took off!" I can't stop myself. Sure enough, the grocery bag is behind the front seat. Another batch of cold ones. No multi-grain, all-pure, hippie nut-bread, though. I ease back into the house with the bag. I wasn't being all that mean because I had politely abstained from checking to see if she drank one on the way back.

I stand there quietly for a second, holding my tongue. Maybe because Dad and Marcy look so happy. Maybe because Dad is drinking the last beer from the first shipment himself. Trish gets up and walks past me, whispering, "Show time!" She turns around and plunks down in Dad's chair at the table, the seat of power.

I want to take the heat off my sliding the new batch of Busch beer into the fridge. "That Camaro..." Five full bottles, one empty. "It's a '69, isn't it?"

"You bet. Thanks for bringing the beer in."

I wink. "Don't mention it."

Dad is watching me ball up the grocery bag with the six-pack carton for the trash can. He goes to the fridge and peers in, snatching out the empty I left in there. I manage to get my foot on the garbage-can pedal just in time for him to wing it in.

"The refrigerator is the center of attention around here," Trish says sweetly. I'm sitting down and she gives me a kick under the table. I look back. Dad has returned to the machine which is not church but awful close to it, and he's pulling out another beer for himself.

"And to top things off," Marcy announces, "it's almost time to fly the Camaro over to the karate studio to pick up Pashy from her class!"

"Karate class!" Trish says. "Far out!"

"Sixties-speak," Marcy beams.

"Solid!" I say.

"Fifties! Well, Johnny?" she says to my father, and believe me, everybody calls him John. "Johnny? You have your children educated!"

It's their mother," Johnny says, missing a chance to plug himself. "Maybe we should hold off on supper for a few minutes if we're going to leave to get Passion."

Marcy catches Dad clicking off the oven.

"It was only on pre-heat, Johnny, I mean..."

"Pre-heat is the hottest thing on there," Trish says. I nod in agreement.

"Well, where's the thermostat for the air-conditioning? It's getting so warm in here." Marcy puts down the tray of junk-food bread she has just buttered.

"It's in the hallway," Dad says meekly. "But we keep it on 78 to save energy, you know, like..."

Marcy was already out in the hall, cranking the AC to Hi-Cool. "If you've got it, flaunt it!" she says, flashing her super-white teeth.

"That's a no-no, Miss Marcy," Trish says, up and heading for the control. My sister has a strong sense of territory, and Dad had to stop her with a chest-high arm-block across the hallway entrance.

"It's an adult world, girl."

"And you're the adult here, right? And you said to keep the thermostat on seventy-eight. No matter what! You said that people who..."

Tricia's words choke off as Dad's iron right hand initiates a shoulder-crushing squeeze.

Marcy butts in. "People who what, Honey?" She's back over there in two leggy strokes. She clamps her hand over Dad's, which is still mashing the juice out of Tricia's meat. I hunker down in my chair, feeling the pain myself. I see the day coming when Trish and I will need to become real friends.

"Come on, Johnny. We could all use a ride in the car."

Johnny loosens the Grip-of-Death. I'm able to relax myself now and I begin to think out loud. "If we go in the Camaro to get Pashy," (I say her name like I'm referring to something sacred) "who's going to drive? Dad said we shouldn't go with anybody who's driving under the influence. Ever." Which would leave me, I was hoping, as the only wise choice.

Marcy got all backed up. "Well, then. What we'll do is Johnny and I'll go and you two kids can lay back here and dig security and comfort! Strap yourselves in on the living-room couch. Buckle up for safety! Or whatever else that turns you on that's safe and decent!"

"Now Marcy...." Dad says quietly. "I don't think..."

"It's okay, Dad!" I say. "I didn't mean it! Really! You guys aren't drunk or anything like that."

"Yet," Trish says.

We all watch Johnny chug-a-lug the rest of his beer and slam the empty down on the counter. He turns on us, eyes darting from one to another, and announces that he will drive.

"The Camaro?" Trish says, looking at me and nodding.

"Marcy?" Dad is looking at her for permission, like a puppy begging for a biscuit. I hate to see it, but Trish giggles.

"Sure! Why don't you guys go, and I'll stay here and keep dinner going!"

"The Camaro?"

"Jeez, Dad." I look at him. "You guys came here together!"

"You must've left our Kia somewhere, Daddy!"

I wink at Marcy. "In the heat of passion, no, I mean, lust, no — I mean..."

"Oh, yeah...." Dad says. "Shut up, David."

"And you two young'uns sit in the back, okay?" Marcy says. "Pashy gets motion sickness in the back seat."

"So do I!" I blurt out before Trish has a chance.

"Well, Passion pukes up green stuff."

Dad turns on his command tone. "Passion sits in the front." He's out the door before we can rally, leaving us to race for the car and fight for our positions in the back. But I outfox Trish by pulling back at the last second and nailing down the front bucket-seat for myself. "Dad, I'll move to the back when we get there."

Tricia grumps. "You didn't give her a goodbye kiss, Daddy."

Our father fumbles with the ignition key. Suddenly the car bursts into life with a roar, and we settle back into our vibrating seats for the big thrill. I dig a bottle cap out from under my ass and give it a quick inspection just before Dad retrofires our new hotrod into the street.

"Pepsi!" I declare, flicking the cap back at Trish. "Must've been the passenger."

"Pashy!" Trish yells. "The new generation!"

Our petty conversation is killed in the neck-snapping blast-off from our home base. I push myself back up in the seat and fight the G's as the perfectly spaced and familiar houses of our neighborhood recede in a dizzying blur. I twist my head to the left and see the tach heading for 6000 before Johnny shifts into second gear. Another neck snap.

"Dad!"

From the back seat comes: "Children against drunk fathers!"

We touch down briefly at the stop sign before burning onto the main drag. I was worried, but proud of us at the same time.

"She let me use it the other day on my run to the trauma center!" Dad is shouting this to the rest of the world. "I've had some practice!"

"We didn't know!"

"Live to die!"

True.... Suddenly Dad slows down — all the way to a crawl. Trish is tapping my shoulder from behind. We're passing by some kids on the sidewalk. They're wearing two-piece white pajamas. Karate troopers. To me they looked like high-tech Ku Klux Klan. Solid state KKK. No tubes to get hot and burn out. They were coming from the karate studio that used to be our hardware store before Wal-Mart.

The Camaro is loping and jerking along. The motor wants to be turned loose again — I can feel it. Trish says: "How will we know which one is her?"

Dad looks proud. "Marcy said Passion's the only one that changes back into her street clothes after class." He swings our machine into the loading zone in front of the building, barely nudging the back bumper of a mother in a shiny-new van loading up on brats. Dad sets the hand-brake and blips the throttle a couple times to enjoy the sound o' power. The mother ahead of us looks back and snarls something, but none of the karate snots on the sidewalk turns a head to check out the car with the macho growl. Boards up their asses. More of them are marching out the front door of the building now. So cool. Little chins up. More girls than I would have thought....

"Flat chested," Trish notes.

"Not all of them, Sis." The older ones were emerging now, like streaming from an alien pod.

"They kill me."

"Not so loud!" Dad says.

"Bet they're not bullet proof."

Dad adds to the philosophy. "One day they'll all have kids of their own, and mortgages...." He sighs.

Hungrily, we wait for the magic moment when Passion will be revealed unto us. I picture the scene back home at this moment: the empty oven turned on red-hot, the AC churning the temp down to a meat-locker, slow-death chill, the eggs with the green lawn-clippings overflowing the mixing bowl, and Johnny's new, hot date passed out at the kitchen table....

I know Dad's lonely — Trish and I are, too.

The rumbling of the Camaro reminds me that all is not lost. This was going to be better than watching TV, anyway. It's just that what we all needed, it seemed to me, was for Dad to find somebody beautiful to look at who is also a neat person — no, I mean somebody who is also intelligent. A mother for us and a buddy for Dad. A real mother. Like on TV commercials where in seconds the mother has this new stuff they're advertising sliding out of the oven and right onto the table with a white table-cloth and everybody is sitting around and smiling and giving thanks and drinking Gallo wine. Except I didn't want a grand-mother type. Real grandmothers can hardly walk. I know. I have friends who have grandmothers actually living with them. Sometimes they can't even make it to the bathroom in time.

Trish is poking me, bringing me back to Earth. I suck in my breath. Passion! Even if she hadn't recognized the car, I would have known. Passion....

"Well, well," Dad says faintly. I swallow hard and wonder how my tongue can dry up so fast. It's not that this girl is built. Really not. Well, I mean, in addition, she was in charge. In charge! Like instead of the front door of the karate school opening up and letting her out, I am seeing a space ship opening up and this beautiful princess stepping out to greet primitive mankind. Tall. Cool. Piercing eyes boring into me as I stumble out of her mother's car to vacate the front seat — her eyes punching through my speechless stare like bullets through cardboard. Full lips, painted, half-open and sucking me in to spit me out as the word "Hi!" tumbles out of mine. I lurch out of her path to the side and my right foot snags on the curb and I go down. Damn! Instinctively I hold my grip on the door and instead of sprawling face down at her feet I manage to pull myself into the back of the car half-way through the fall. As I claw my way off Tricia, who had switched sides to be a bitch, I retracted my twisted feet just in time for Passion to float down into her throne in the front. She turns and looks back at us, offering her hand between the seats. Long, curving, vampire-red nails. Perfect nails. Long. Curving. Vampire red....

"I'm Pashy," she's says in this low, sultry voice. "Daughter of Marcella."

I haul myself upright and take the sacred hand. My eyes meet hers once more in a feeble attempt to even up the score so far. I might as well have tried to hurl marshmallows through boiler plate. Her hand is electric and I give it my most meaningful, gentle but firm squeeze. My brain, already on Emergency Power, is scrambling for suitable words.

"David," I say manfully.

"I am Tricia," my sister says evenly. "Daughter of Johnny."

"I am John." Dad says.

To my relief we all laugh. Dad taps the throttle of the old but hot Camaro and lets the engine rip for a second. I wished, then, that I were driving. With Passion at my side. Forget Trish. Forget Dad. Forget Marcy....

We pull out from the curb and Dad makes a gentle U-turn. Trish says something quietly in my ear about how Dad is always complaining about other people making U-turns but I couldn't relate to that just then. I was locked into the oblique view of Passion's noble head. I was consumed. It was love. True love. No one else would ever do. My future was written.

Bleeding through the rapture was my father's voice. Something like: "Well, daughter of Marcy — I was under the impression that you were younger."

"Me, too." Trish said.

"I am thirteen."

Dad said: "Thirteen? Thirteen what?"

Trish snickered. I was beginning to come back. I could feel my feet in my sneakers, and wiggle my toes. I could hear the Camaro rumbling along at a sedate speed toward home. I could smell Passion's perfume — or was it her aura — like the clean, alive, electric scent of the air after a thunderstorm with a hint of Mom's lingerie drawer. I sucked in a deep breath of this goddess. Love.... Dear Lord, Thy works are great!

Her words poured like honey. "Where's Marcella?" the Daughter of Marcella said.

"Your mother's at our place — cooking," Dad says. "You don't call her mother? Or mom?"

"Or mommy?" Precious Trish.

"Revenge for naming me Passion." Her low, velvet voice turned out a melody of laughter as she tilted her head back. Her neck was beautiful. Exquisite. She was a swan. With wonder and pain, my soul drank of her beauty.

"I think your name is unique," Dad is saying. "It stimulates interest and, uhhh..."

"It invokes lust," Passion says.

"That's neat!" Trish says.

"I like your name," I said. I'd wanted to say: I love your name!

"It invokes lust. And here I am, just trying to cope with being thirteen. Really!"

"Thirteen what?" Dad asked again, which wasn't all that funny.

"Thirteen units," Passion replied easily. She and I both laughed at that one. She was beautiful and intelligent! And she had turned her head and was looking at me with the faintest of smiles.

"You practiced that smile in front of the mirror," I said, surprising myself. "You must've seen the original at the Louvre."

"Oh, don't mind the genius here," Dad had to say.

"I do practice my Mona Lisa smile before the mirror!" Her eyes were now fixed into mine. "Our mirror has a gold frame around it, too. Marcella got it at a flea market. With a bad check. She had to call the man up the next morning and beg him not to deposit it right away." Passion was still looking at me and I was still drinking her in. We were pulling into our driveway. The motor shut down. Dad's door opened and he was out, slamming the door shut before Tricia could get to it.

"I can't get out!" Trish grumped, stamping her foot and breaking the spell.

Passion slid out and held her door open. Trish scampered over me and I followed her out of the back. I watched her trot after Dad toward the house, her playsuit flashing moon.

"How old is she?"

"Fourteen." My brain boggled with the realization that my sister was a year older than the object of everything I had ever desired in a woman. "Years," I added.

"Oh, yesssss...." Passion reached for my hand.

She's wants to hold my hand!

She is saying: "I'm really very shy but, well, this is a new place for me." She gives my hand a gentle but lingering squeeze.

"I'm the shy one," I blurt. I squeeze back. Get a grip! "I'll just have to overcome it." Oh, I was proud of myself for that one. But in fact I was terrified to the bone. A long pause followed and I scrambled to fill it. "My mother's not here. She drinks a lot and my father gave her a choice. So she split. For good, I think...." What to do with her hand?

"My mother drinks, too. All the time! I probably shouldn't have told you that, but..."

"I understand." Now we were holding both hands, facing each other, still in the driveway. I swallowed hard and hoped she didn't notice.

"My parents split up, too. Divorce. Well, well...."

"Well well is what I use sometimes, too." Why did I have to say that!? She catches me looking down, too — I mean, looking her over. "Well, well, I say again, breaking into a laugh, saving myself (I hope). We look at our hands and start bouncing them up-and-down. Then, as if on cue, we both stepped back a little, still holding on, looking into each other's eyes.

"Well, well...."

"Yeah...."

"Hmmm!"

"What can I say...."

"Yeah...."

Somebody had to do it — break this high-level dialogue. "I think somebody's going to have to come out here and get us. To break the spell!" I was attempting to look back with equal power into her steady gaze.

"Pashy! What are you doing?"

"The serenity shattered by Marcella," Passion says slowly, her voice low and seductive. Pure maple syrup.

I say, "Should I stay here and wait — to see if my parent remembers me?"

Passion broke our hand-clasp and turned toward the house, then looked back at me. In a hoarse whisper, she says: "I'm really fifteen and I'm not stupid but I flunked two grades in school and that's Mom's excuse but you didn't hear it from me!"

She was gone. For a moment, I could hear the lawn-mower from a couple doors down the street. It would drone along steadily and then hit stuff, like you could hear sprinkler heads clanking into the blade and slowing it down — like when Mom would insist on cutting our grass herself after she'd been drinking Saturday morning. Suddenly I heard this big *clang!* and the neighborhood went silent. Silent except for the inside of my head, that is. This voice of an angel kept saying: I'm really fifteen. I'm really fifteen....

And then my parent remembered me, and called from the back door. And I understood. It was OK if Marcy wanted to call him "Johnny". They saw something in each other. Who was I to question the power of such things?

And who knows what desires had been aroused in this man, my father, when I was conceived?

Off in the distance the lawn-mower started up again. It didn't sound as good as before, though, and it died. *silence....* And then Passion was beside me, taking my hand again, tugging me toward the back door.

"David? They have decided we all need to be inside while dinner progresses. I guess because progress is going to be all uphill!" She laughed and kept on tugging me along as I pretended to drag my feet. God did love me after all! All of my life's misfortunes to this point had been merely a test. And I'd passed. I had been found worthy. And this angel in human flesh was my reward. I decided right then to stop playing sick on Sunday mornings. I would go to church willingly. I believed. Heaven had sent me the most wondrous woman ever made. Not in my dreams but here. Here on Earth! And she was leading me into my own house, into my own kitchen! Oh, how wonderful is her hair! The flash of her smile! Her body the fulfillment of my wildest dreams! Her voice...

"And I'm intelligent," she said, laughing. "Just like you!"

"And a mind reader!"

"I flunked because I was cutting classes all the time."

"A mind reader."

"ESP — you believe in it?" Passion suddenly stopped tugging at me and we bumped into each other, you know, her chest and my arm, just a little, by accident, when she stopped.

"Sorry," I said instinctively, immediately wishing my mouth could be cool instead of blurting out everything before I had time to think. I stepped back just enough to relieve this elbow contact with ecstasy but she moved with me and hooked her arm under mine to draw me closer. My heart hammered up while the sane part of me tried to regain control of whatever systems I had left. But the only signals allowed access to my brain at this point were coming from about ten square inches of pressure against my upper arm: warm full rich plump Nothing in my girlie-magazine literature had prepared me for this!

"Marcella makes me take birth control pills. I think that's why they're so, you know, so...."

"You? Lost for words? Ha!" I gave her wrist a squeeze when what I really wanted to do was palpate the fruit.

"Filled out."

"Ripe."

"Ripe."

I wanted to look down and let my eyes roam around there, but I couldn't.

"Ripe with fruit."

"Heavy with fruit."

"Laden."

"Burgeoning." We laughed, and looked into each other's eyes again.

I couldn't believe the level of this conversation — and my luck! "Sunkist ripe," I said, referring to the little logo printed on the otherwise plain, light-blue, slightly too small T-shirt covering the fruit from Hell. *Sunkist....*

"And I'm a virgin! But she makes me take the pills anyway so I don't embarrass her one day. Hell, I'd be scared, you know, to do it. Catch something. Know why I'm telling you this?"

My mind jammed. I made a start for the back door but her arm was still hooked into mine and she hauled me back. "You believe I'm a virgin, don't you?"

She didn't give me a chance to compute. "I — well, sure!"

"You better! You know why I'm telling you this, David?"

Her eyes were looking right through mine and scraping the back of my skull. A real control freak. I pictured her controlling me, standing over me, forcing me to perform unnatural acts.

"I'm telling you because I think you are a, well — you're a virgin, too. Right? Am I right? Ha ha! I'm right! And Marcella told me your father told her you had a genius IQ. Right? A genius IQ?" Her arm tightened around mine.

"Yeah, well...." I could handle the genius part. Graduate early from college and go directly to McDonald's. Big deal. Smart and fifteen. So smart I was afraid of girls. Girls, women, females, foxes — all I ever think about lately. Friends at school are continually bragging about their scores. Being the youngest in my class doesn't help, either. I've been wanting a girl bad. I lie awake for hours and dream about what she'd feel like all wrapped around me, nude. What she'd feel like inside. What it would be like to reach into her blouse and pull the fruits out and feel of them. Squeeze them and kiss them and feel of them for so long that the memory will last forever. But people tell you, hey, wait until you're older and you're ready for the responsibilities. Or they say, don't forget about AIDS! How can I forget? Forgetting's not it! So I die later! Skip old age! By-pass the nursing home stuff, right?

I tell myself I'm simply waiting for the right girl to come along. Casual sex doesn't pay — they're right. I am doing the right thing. But deep down inside I know better. I want to get laid. I want to get laid now. Bad. I am a virgin because I'm chicken. Chicken!

"It scares me," Passion is saying.

I must have jumped, or twitched. She turns me loose and steps back. "You look a little gray around the gills, David."

"Heh! Yeah, well, I'm not used to getting right into the heavy stuff with someone I just met. You're a — surprise attack! So to speak, ha ha...." I'm nodding my head, pleased with myself once again. I was handling this.

We began to move toward the back door but stopped when we got there. The door opens. It's Johnny. Beer in hand. Standing in the doorway staring at us — and then, quite frankly, staring at Passion. "Would a little cold water with the garden hose do it?" He laughed.

Passion looked peeved. After giving Dad a quick glance, she continues our conversation as if he weren't there. "On the other hand, Marcella doesn't need to take the pill 'cause she's been fixed. Still has her ovaries, though. All the precious hormones intact. But no incubator. No muss, no fuss. Ready to trot all thirty days of the month!"

Dad looked shocked. "Passion! Thirteen? God help us!"

"We're religious," I explained. Dad moved quickly but I dodged and missed his fatal shoulder clamp by inches.

"I'll explain that!" Marcy said, running up behind Dad. "The thirteen, I mean. And Passion's big mouth! I send her to self-defense classes to learn discipline —

not just how to fight. Confidence building. How to crumble people with an attitude, with a mere word. So what does she do? She practices on her own family! On her own mother!"

"They teach us to abstain from things harmful, like alcohol." Passion slipped past Dad and Marcy and disappeared into the house.

Dad's shoulders were slumped. He looked at me. "You all right?"

"Yeah.... Are you?'

"I'm not sure...." His voice trailed off. Then he straightened up. "Come on inside now. I need a backup."

"We're both going to need backup, Pop." We laughed and bumbled into our kitchen. Father and son.

The heat was stifling and there was a burny smell. Marcy and Trish were be-bopping around to the rap music on the kitchen boom-box, and Passion had seated herself on Dad's high, antique stool in the corner. She was facing everybody like an eagle on her perch. So beautiful. So in control! She had kicked her sandals off and I would have willingly dropped to my knees and kissed her toes, her feet were so fine. The toes so perfect and the nails painted to blood-red perfection.

"The garlic-bread burned," Marcy said, panting. "And the omelets."

"And the air-conditioner," Passion said.

Trish was still bopping around. "The air-conditioning never breaks down at Burger King!"

I turned the AC control to Off and headed for the stairs to the basement. Man of the house. I stopped, as if I just had a second thought. "Come on, Pash. Let's go down and check the circuit breakers."

"You have a basement?" Passion slid off the stool and followed me bare-footed down the basement stairs. But before I could get to the fuse box she caught me and turned me around. I hadn't turned the lights on but it wasn't so dark I couldn't see her. My heart pounded up as she pulled me close. Our chests touched.

"Let them feel the heat up there," she whispered, "while we feel the heat down here."

Thank God for pushy females! I bend my head close to hers, moving in. Terrified or not, it was going to happen! We were going to kiss! Our lips were going to touch! I was on the threshold of tasting the forbidden fruit of her mouth! Parting my lips ever so slightly, I...

"Yeeeech!" She shoved me away hard and then wiped her mouth with the back of her hand. "Your breath!"

"I..."

"Don't you ever brush your teeth?"

I felt like I'd been punched in the gut. I couldn't breathe. My stomach burned. I could feel my ears turning red in the darkness. "I, uh...."

"Forget it, David! Your breath is — nauseating!"

I swallowed. I wanted to die. Finally, I took a deep breath and headed for the fuse box. Her rejection was crushing me and I had to push myself to keep going. With the flashlight that Dad kept there, I scanned the breakers for #8. It was tripped. I flipped it back to ON.

"My mother won't let me near the fuse box," Passion said from somewhere behind me. Like nothing had happened. I swallowed hard again and carefully closed the gray metal door of the box. Somehow I was able to turn and face her but not her eyes, or the precious lips which had almost been mine. My head was shaking and I was grateful for the dark. As I faced her, she backed away from me.

"Well, I'm sorry," she said, but I keep myself clean. You must have decaying food in your mouth — between your teeth, you know, the cracks between. If we would kiss, well, I mean, chunks of that rotting stuff would fall off your teeth and get into my mouth and..."

I walked around and past her, hoping the redness of my burning ears was not noticeable. As I headed up the stairs I felt a tear coming but I made like I had to scratch my head and caught the tear with my thumb. I could hear her bare feet padding up the stairs behind me and I pictured those feet for a second, her bare toes.... I pictured her lips, her beautiful face, her

Sunkist shirt bobbing up-and-down (I was sure) behind me, her mouth....

"...make me retch! You ever smell a dead animal, David? Or meat when it goes bad in the refrigerator? When Marcella bought the Camaro, the check to the electric company bounced and they shut off our current for a while and everything in the fridge..."

I walked into the kitchen and pulled out a chair at the table, then had to get back up again because I forgot that it was probably OK now to switch the AC back on. Passion was still talking. Dad and Marcy and Trish were all sitting there, looking at us and looking dumb. I set the AC to 78 and heard the unit click on.

"...and everything in the fridge spoiled. Well, not everything. The bacon was still sort of okay. But the hamburger meat — yeeech! I almost threw up when I sniffed it. It smelled just like your breath!"

"Passion!" Marcy yelled. She sounded drunk. Like Mom used to sound when she was cooking supper.

I faced Passion and spoke with my lips as closed as possible. "It didn't smell like burned food?"

"David!" Dad yelled. He sounded drunk, too. A little, anyway.

"It never smells burny at Burger King!" Trish said.

"Floss," Passion is saying. "The un-waxed kind. After every meal, same as brushing. I floss after brushing but Marcella flosses before."

"Before passing out, or before brushing." I was able to look her in the eye again, even though my head was still shaking. She was back up on the stool — her eagle perch.

"David!" Dad barks again.

Trish begins humming the tune from the latest Burger King commercial. Marcy was looking at me from her slouched-over position at the table, eyes half open and glazing over. Suddenly her chin slips off the palm of her hand and she has to scramble for balance.

Tell you what," Dad says, using his happy tone. "Marcy's not feeling well, and dinner's spoiled, so why don't we get her comfortable on the couch and then the rest of us go down to Burger King!"

"The Camaro!" Trish squeals. "Burger King! All - O - Us!"

Passion catches me running my tongue over my teeth, hunting for food particles.

Trish is up on her feet, flashing around in her Day-Glo playsuit. "Can we call Mommy? See if she wants to come, too?"

"Not today," Dad said.

I pick up on it. "Next time then?" I regretted saying that but I wanted to cut Marcy and Passion.

"Sure, Son."

Marcy shot Dad a look and tried to get up. Dad and I caught her by the arms and headed her for the living-room. When we got back Passion was still on her stool. She was staring out the window at the back yard. It seemed to me a good time to ease down to the bathroom to brush my teeth. And from now on it would be after every meal. After every snack. And I'd floss. For the rest of my life.

Dad looks at Passion. "Where's Trish?"

"Telephone." Bored eyes, looking out the window.

On the way to the bathroom I stop to hear what Trish is saying to Mom. From the kitchen I can hear Dad trying crank up a conversation with Passion, and I think I hear that velvet voice say: "I'm really seventeen, but..."

"But Mommy!" Trish is saying. "They say on TV that you can't even have just one! You have to quit forever! Not one, teeny little drink! Wait! Here's David! He'll tell you!"

I take the phone. *Seventeen...?* "Mom? I miss you." That sounded sort of dumb but it was the truth.

"Hi, David! I love you, too!"

She doesn't sound the least bit drunk. "Did you quit?"

"No.... I cut down. To two a day. I cut down because I don't believe I should have to, you know, do without completely. You know."

"Yeah, I know. Mom..."

"I'm tough, David. I can do it. I am doing it."

"Yeah, but for how long?"

"David — forever, I hope. Today I had my after-work beer and I didn't even feel like having the second one. That's a first! When can I see you? Trish says you guys are having quite an experience today."

"Yeah. But I'm doing okay." Trish is clawing at me for the phone and I back-hand her a swat. "Trish can't wait her turn."

"It was my turn!"

Dad is standing next to us now and he places his gentle clamp on my shoulder — ready to escalate. "Mom, Dad wants to talk."

We let Dad run on-and-on, the way he always does when he has Mom on the phone and she's sober. I peer into the living-room at Marcy's still body. I move in a little closer. She's breathing, but almost imperceptibly. She looks so peaceful now. Even beautiful. I remember how reverently Dad had taken off her clogs and placed them side-by-side next to the couch. It was what I would have done.

Would I have removed Mom's old floppy slippers with the same care and affection? Would Dad? I head down the hall for the bathroom. It wasn't Mom's fault that we didn't know what we wanted. But it wasn't our fault, either.

Passion had decided to stay with her mother in the living-room and we would bring her back a take-out from Burger King. The thought that both of them would be staying overnight in our house thrilled me, but there was something missing now.

"Cheer up, guys!" Dad said when we got into the Camaro. "We've got a great team, and it's our ball!"

"Yeah," I said. "What game are we playing?"

"There's only one game, Son." Dad turned and gave me a strange look.

"Come on! Crank 'er up and let's go," Trish said. "I'm not having a problem!"

"That's because you're not grown up yet," Dad said to her while he looked at me. He was smiling, and for the first time I could see into my father's eyes. •

JOHN AALBORG

Furby Mountain Florida

Shortly before all this happened, when Brenda was still with him, Ralph saw a fellow truck-driver sneaking a Furby into a truckstop motel. A Furby is a cute, furry, battery-operated, talking-toy animal — popular a few years ago but still available — with a tiny, interactive computer inside. The trucker, a middle-aged, burly guy, had the Furby partly covered with his jacket as he tried to get both his suitcase and the stowaway under his arm through the doorway to his room. When he saw Ralph spot the Furby's ears poking out from the opening in his jacket, he turned to the side to hide it. Ralph wanted to say, "Hey, who cares? You're still a man, right?"

On the other hand, if it were me ....

§

They didn't even hold up the funeral for him, well, typical, her family, Ralph thought, wiping the tears away with one of the new hankie/bandannas Brenda had bought him just a few weeks back. The grief was paralyzing and he wasn't sure he could go on. He had just finished a run from Vancouver all the way to

Miami with a drop in Cleveland, and the last two times he had called-in the boss's kids dropped the ball on the messages they were supposed to relay. It was a small outfit with only three other rigs, and the owner was on the road most of the time himself. Brenda was supposed to be driving her car to Atlanta during this trip, to vacation with her parents, and since Ralph usually avoided calling her family....

He found out about the accident just before the Miami drop, and the Cuban consignee did the best he could, giving Ralph his cell-phone — "Long distance? No problem!" — and even had his men sweep off the flatbed and roll up the tarps for him. So grief-stricken he could barely drive away, and exhausted, Ralph found himself, without remembering the drive out of Miami, pulling the empty truck into the Seminole Travel Plaza west of Ft. Lauderdale just before dark. Only another hour or so up Hwy-27 toward Lake Okeechobee and he could make it home, but without Brenda there....

He sipped a Corona at the outdoor chickee bar, then ordered a Heineken, Brenda's favorite beer, and decided he'd be better off in the truck-sleeper tonight. Everybody was paying attention to the Hispanic barmaid, so pretty and almost a carbon copy of Brenda — especially with the dappled light from the strings of colored bulbs coming on now all over the thatched roof. When she pushed the Heineken toward him, "No glass, right?", she sounded like Brenda but with an accent, and she flashed Brenda's easy, bright smile. When she turned away Ralph was fighting back another tear. Brenda was a lot younger than Ralph when they married, which seemed to be the main problem with her family. Plus the fact he was an over-the-road trucker while her father was an engineer with some twenty electronic inventions pulling in major bacon. They resented her going on runs with him. "No life on the road, that flatbed truck, for a girl with a future." Brenda enjoyed the life, though, and had become as good with the tarps and winches and chain-binders as any male trucker.

A driver plunked onto the next stool. "You look like you got run over with your own truck, furby-man." He was thin, old, and brown-skinned, wearing wire-frame bifocals and a worn, black T-shirt from Mike's Truck Pavilion on Virginia Beach — Ralph owned a shirt just like it — with the illustration and the caption: "If you can't run with the big dogs, stay on the porch!"

"Gimme a Bud, baby! No glass, no glass. So pretty! So fine you are!" The driver nudged Ralph with an elbow. "She beautiful or what!?"

"I can't get into that right now."

"I see that, furby-man."

"Furby man?"

"I seen it in your cab. You pulled in next to me when I was catchin' up my paper. The tan Pete with the forty-eight foot garbage wagon? That's me."

"Oh, yeah.... Big hydraulic-oil tank where the sleeper should be."

"Hey, I'm home every night."

"But first you come here and check out the babes... Never mind."

"I live with my mother. I'm strictly PG-13."

"I had a bad day."

"They all bad. No, they all good. It's all in your head."

"When bears use the bathroom."

"No, true!"

"My wife got killed while I was away. Is that in my head?"

"Aw! Oh, man, I'm sorry. So sorry."

"They had her in the ground before I even knew about it."

"Aw. Terrible. I'm sorry."

 They both watched the barmaid — for different reasons — so foxy, so lively.

"The jukebox is busted," they heard her say, down at the other end. The darkening sky flashing through the lower fringes of the roof-thatch — heat lightening — and a cool breeze blowing up but no rain. The other patrons, mostly drivers, were fairly quiet for a South Florida, outdoor bar scene.

"But the Furby's yours, right? Not a present? My name's Jamie. Not in a box, you know, you have it sitting there so it can look out the windshield like it's real or something. I know. So it can see out? I'm sorry.

Not a good time to talk." Jamie swiveled away and fixed on the barmaid again. Her long, purple fingernails poking at the register to ring up a drink. Silent for a moment, he turned back to Ralph. "I know all about Furbies. My son, Little-J, he's addicted to 'em and he's full grown! Thinks they can think. It's all programmed in, I tell 'im. He knows it. He don' want to hear it. They're real, he says."

"That's what Brenda says. Said.... It's her Furby. The one in my cab."

"I'm sorry. Yeah. My son, he fixes 'em — you can't hardly find 'em anymore — he takes 'em apart, I mean, he knows they got a computer chip for a brain, some chip memory, you know. Then he puts 'em back together and says they're real. It's just a mechanical toy with some fur around it and four AA batteries. Listen, if I smack it a good one with my fist, it stops working, right? Mechanical. Not real."

"If you smack a man hard enough he quits working."

"Oh. Yeah.... But his soul is still alive. Oh, I see where you're goin'."

"I wasn't going nowhere with that," Ralph said, finally turning and taking in a good look at this other driver, looked like Sammy Davis Jr. with gray hair instead of black. Neat looking guy.... "Mine's broken," Ralph said. I promised Brenda I knew where to get him fixed and I'd bring him back, CB shop up near the

Newcomerstown truckstop in Ohio, but the man was on vacation when I stopped."

"So your Furby's broke but you let him look out the windshield anyway. Cool. Yeah, don' send 'em out to get fixed. They might send a refurbished one back. My son calls 'em re-furbs, get it? Refurbs? An' maybe you don' always get back the same one. Even if they send one back the same color, your old lady would know if it was different. They switched a blind guy's Furby one time and he knew right away. Different personality. And some talk faster than others, and they do different stuff depending how you bring em up."

The barmaid moved up to them. "You talking about my Furby?" Ralph turned to her and jumped, she was so close — so much like Brenda — flashier, though, all that lipstick and that Latin accent. She said, "I don't bring him here no more. Customers mess him up. I want to get another one. They talk to each other, you know, but the stores, well, the Furbies are off the shelves."

Jamie said: "I seen some before Christmas last year somewhere. They're out of date, but it's adults want 'em now but you don' hear about it 'cause they's embarrassed about it, you know, a toy. You can get 'em on the internet, too. Then the old people gotta have two so the other Furby don' get lonely. Ever hear two Furbies together? It's weird. It's ... ungodly!"

"Adults?" Ralph said.

"Truckers got 'em. You got one!"

"It's my wife's."

The barmaid said, "She an adult? Your wife?" She laughed and moved down the bar.

"She's a smarty, that one," Jamie said. "Mmmmmm - mmmmmm!"

"Just a toy...."

"Her? Oh! Yeah, well.... Little-J will fix yours. He s'pose to meet me here any minute. He can look at it right here."

"I don't want to bring Brenda's furb in here."

"Oh. Normally he don' do pickup and delivery but..."

"Not in here. Some drunk will want to pick him up, you know, and..."

"...he goes by the nursin' homes. He does those. P & D's for the old people. Just a toy, huh?"

"A little, mindless robot." Ralph was feeling the crush of Brenda being gone forever, and this other guy didn't get it. "I gotta go."

"He stop by the nursin' homes at night sometime, after work. Halls dark. Lights out. Maybe one nurse roamin' around.... Real quiet, you see, 'cept for now, lately, you can hear these used, freebie Furbies — folks donate 'em — through the doors at night, he says, when the old folks s'pose to be sleepin'. They say: 'Me happy! Me love you! Me hungry! Pet me again!'" Jamie had changed his voice to tiny-and-loveable, like a little kid, like a Furby. "They say: 'No light! Me sleepy!'"

Ralph collected his change but left a dollar, and started off his stool.

"Wait! Little-J be here any minute now. You got a pickup tomorrow?"

"I'm taking time off."

"Ever been up on the Pompano Beach landfill in a big truck? It's a trip! Take your mind off..."

"No. No, no...."

§

Jamie's son, Little-J, turned out to be much younger than Ralph expected, under twenty anyway, and huge. Fish-belly white with a smooth head shaved to the bone. Blond eyebrows festooned with golden rings and ears pierced with safety pins. Bright-blue eyes.... His dark-skinned father, looking even smaller and thinner now, was obviously proud of his son as he stood dwarfed in his shadow. "This is my boy, Little-J. Ain' he beautiful? You should see his mother!"

"Dad...."

After a manly handshake, Ralph got Brenda's Furby out of the truck and sat it down carefully on a picnic table near the lighted parking area. Little-J ambled over there like a big polar bear, in slouchy khakis. The furb's eyes were closed.

"Seems awful heavy. What's his name?"

"Furb."

"Ain't they all. Must be special batteries, the weight. You ever check 'em?"

"Yeah. Anyway, Brenda always knew when the batteries were still good. She said Furb wasn't acting right. She's said she'd been feeding him regular, and playing with him, you know, so he doesn't get depressed and get sick. It's not the batteries."

"Hmmmm...."

"She said on the day he didn't seem right he was quiet for a minute, and then he said, 'Me love you', and then he was gone."

Little-J was tilting him from side-to-side but the Furby wouldn't wake up. Eyes still closed, quiet....

"I told her, 'It's just a little robot, Honey. It doesn't know when it's been fed, or how long it's been asleep.' But before that, when she was on National Guard duty, I told her I'd take Furb along in the truck and take care of him, and Brenda said: 'Be sure to get Furb up and feed him every day,' you know, she said, 'You will, won't you? For me?'" Ralph choked up a little but went on. "Anyway, I never got him out of the box — the little bed she made for him — the whole trip. And when I finally got home Brenda was back, so I rumpled his bedding a little to make it look like I been getting him out and feeding him all along, you know, hell, they don't really eat, you just put a spoon up to their mouth, so what's the difference, right? So I brought it in the house and when she wiggled it to wake it up, Furb said, 'Cock-a-doodle-do! Me hungry! Hmmmmmmm, big sleep! Me sleep long time!'"

§

After Jamie's first, loaded trailer pickup the next morning, in Florida City, they headed the garbage-load out toward Pompano and pulled off at the end of the Sawgrass Expressway on Sample Road — a full-bore road race — and two lights and two turns later they were jamming it inside a row of garbage trucks as fast as traffic would permit. Some of them were eighteens like Jamie's but most were dumpster snatchers or big city-trucks with the tilt-backs. While waiting on the scales for his weight, Jamie reached outside for his rubber boots. "Some drivers don' care about getting dirt an' that smell inside the cab but you gotta wonder what kind of chicks they score, too." After spreading some old newspapers on the floor on both sides, he whipped the rig back onto the road and followed the arrows.

"Some days they change the route up the mountain." Jamie shouted above the racket, his window down. "On a rainy day, if you slow down, the trucks behind'll try to pass 'cause nobody wants to get stuck in the mud. An' way at the top they try to get ahead of you to dump." After they made the crest, Ralph looked out over the flat, mesa-like top — as big as an airfield — and the spotters: foreign-looking dudes wearing head-rags and swinging axe-handles, using them for pointers. It was another planet up here.

"They the masters here!" Jamie shouted, roaring right up to one of the spotters in low gear, hoping he wouldn't have to stop before the man pointed him to a dump target. "Yup, they rule up here. No shortage of burial ground, neither!"

Ralph winced. *Burial ground....*

The spotter swung the axe-handle in an arc to indicate the turn and dump spot.

"Differential lock an' double-low an' we can't stop now or we sink right in this mush!" Jamie made the circle with the rig toiling through the muck — the turbo on the big Caterpillar engine screaming — then stopped and dropped the rig into reverse during the rock-back. "Look at that dumpster truck sneakin' up your side. We ain't stoppin' for him! We take stuff like that personal up here, furby-man."

Ralph watched the mirror on his side as they backed, and saw two workers with rakes scurrying to get out of the way, and a huge bulldozer, taller than the truck, making a split-second run right behind them. Jamie kept the hammer down. "Garbage pinball, furby-man!"

Another eighteen was now backing alongside them on Jamie's side, and the bulldozer got out of the way just in time.

"Don't want to get stuck now!" Jamie, still shouting and obviously enjoying his job. "When we get out, the ground be movin' — don' fall — it be undulatin'! You fall, you better claw your way outta there. They got what they call The Phantom up here. A phantom driver. Incognito, like. He stay outta sight. The Phantom know how to drive any kind of truck. If a driver fall and get buried accidental, The Phantom jumps in his rig an' completes the dump and then he parks it on the 'rimeter over there. Later on somebody notices the truck abandoned an' they call the company, an' the company think, well, the driver got mad an' walked off the job, you know, 'cause a lot of the new hires can't take it an' they quit."

In position finally, Jamie turned to see if Ralph was buying any of his mythology. He jumped down and headed toward the back of the tractor, still shouting. "Rich people throw good stuff out all the time so keep your eye out for Furbies. An' don' step on no dead bodies but if you see an arm sticking up with a Rolex on it, go for it." Jamie watched Ralph get out and sink past his ankles in the mush. "'Specially if it's still ticking!"

The noise was intimidating and with so many other trucks backing in, dumping, and pulling out, the spongy top of the mountain was rolling like a waterbed. Ralph picked his way carefully to keep from tripping over old window frames, and mattresses sprouting springs, and puffed-up, plump, disposable diapers ready to explode. They made it to the back of the trailer alive and Ralph helped Jamie roll back the last eight feet of tarpaulin, and wing-nut out the six, one-inch door-bolts.

"When the last bolt pops, jump out of the way! Liquid component!"

Ralph barely had to time to react and just missed getting doused with the "liquid component" of the load as the huge door swung open. Two wild-eyed raccoons, trapped in the trailer all night, jumped out and landed running, circling wildly and switching directions, with no place to hide.

Jamie hollered: "Some drivers try to kill 'em but I figure we human animals don' know where we headed neither, when you think about it."

§

That night, in his sleeper again at the truckstop — dreading going home and finding it empty — Ralph had a nightmare. He seemed to be driving up the coast in the dark — no moon — and suddenly, up ahead where something like that shouldn't be, he saw a huge, glowing, electrified mesa rearing up above the skyline from the normally flat, near sea-level, South Florida landscape. The Pompano Beach landfill at night was a megalithic, lighted, flat-topped mountain, awesome and terrifying to behold. The city all around was quiet but at the top of the man-made monster, bulldozers were roaring and clanking in big arcs to flatten out the deposits made during the day. It was humid and rank-smelling up there, and the ground was hot as Ralph found himself stumbling around in rubber boots, trying to stay out of the way of the dozers and the banks of floodlights glaring over the works. He came upon a crew down in a deep trench — a network of pipes down there — "Get away, man! We got methane leaks!" Methane gas.... "See that town down there? That's their electricity! Generator uses methane power! That's why the ground is so hot! Decomposing! It's ready to blow! Get out of here!"

Ralph backed away from the trench and out of the bright lights on stands glaring like robots with dozens of blazing eyes. From behind him he heard more shouts. "Another leak! Over Here! Move the lights!" A floodlight swept past him and Ralph struggled to get away faster, the decomposing, hot trash sucking at his boots. Then he saw them, rising up in the darkness on the far side. Climbing up over the perimeter of the mesa were children, like ghosts. Poor kids in rags, carrying long poles. Dim flashlights flickering here and there, the kids stopping to probe the ground. Their voices were tiny but excited. "I smell it!" one of them said. "Methane! Over here!" The group moved toward him and Ralph could see that a couple of them were quite small. He stopped and watched them tap a pipe into the ground. They began to toss lighted matches down it. Varooooomph! Booooomph! The ground flashed and boiled up on both sides. The kids stopped and cupped their ears, turning this way and that. They were listening for little Furby voices.

"Hmmmmmmmmmmmm! Big sleep!"

"W-o-o-o-o-o-o-o-oh!

"Me hungry!"

"Party! W-e-e-e-e-e!"

The children split up toward the directions of the sounds.

"Found 'im!"

"I got one!"

"Oh, another one!"

§

In the bleak, pre-dawn silence a nearby diesel cranked up, and at another part of the lot, air-brakes released and a stiff gearbox engaged. A few drivers heading out early. It was time for Ralph to crank up and get home and face it: the empty house, the loneliness, the long OTR runs where Brenda would never be riding with him again....

After forcing himself into his routine and making up the bunk, Ralph carefully turned back the cloth over Furby's sleeper-box and lifted him out, hoping that he was still okay after Little-J's repair the evening before. Not ready to wake Furb up just yet, Ralph slid behind the wheel of his rig as daybreak began to take over from the parking lot's spotty lighting. He watched a driver and his wife — looked more like a girlfriend — cross the lot to their rig, a take-out food box from the restaurant in the young lady's hand and a white, bulldog puppy in the man's arms. Farther down the lot another, older couple was easing themselves to the pavement from a gleaming-yellow, Kenworth tractor, the gray-haired woman waiting for the driver, holding out her hand to help him down, the two of them now hand-in-hand and stiffly heading for the building. Single drivers were appearing now, either heading toward the building or toward their units, not looking at all happy. It was a lonely life on the road.

Ralph reached for his sunglasses, tilted the seat back, and nodded off. After a while, his eyes opened to a perfect, bright day. How long had he been sitting there with little Furb in his lap? He dug a tiny, silver spoon from his shirt pocket.

"Here's his spoon," Brenda had said. "Furb's special, pretend-feed spoon".

"Well, here goes," Ralph said aloud. He tilted the Furby to wake him. He would feed him, for Brenda, even if everybody in the world could see. He would feed him because Furb was hungry.

Furb opened his eyes. "Cock-a-doodle-do!," he said. "Me hungry!" •

Exile

When Harry cut the outboard, the sudden quiet and isolation of the overgrown river-landing weighed in with the still and humid air. There were three of them, and Carlos jumped out first after the boat clunked into the near piling.

Harry held a finger to his lips. "She's probably gone now but we'll be quiet anyway, okay?" He never could tell how much English the two teenagers understood. "My second wife. Ex wife. The jitney usually picks her up for the day. The county van. Out at her mailbox on the road. You can't see the road from here."

Tina nodded her head vigorously and smeared a dog-fly which had landed on her forearm. Harry wished their mother was along on this trip. Briza. She would slip into his small apartment occasionally, in the middle of the night, and sometimes he would know even before he could hear her pass-key fumbling in the lock — as if he had been able to read her thoughts from her efficiency down near the laundry room at the other end of the motel. Harry would pretend to be asleep and let her wake him with her pleasant ways. Such dark skin and long, straight, black hair pinned back with barrettes. Two broken teeth and another missing. A tall lady for a Salvadoran illegal. She would feed him her peculiar, tough breasts one at a time, smoothing back his graying hair with her fingers. Briza.... Never asked for money until the next day sometime, and she always told him what it was for.

Tina was much lighter than her mother, with flecks of green in her gray eyes. Wild, strawberry-blond hair, long and showy. Carlos much darker, with full, well-defined lips and a strong chin and short, black, kinky hair. Briza had told Harry she was married at thirteen. Pregnant at thirteen. Another time she told him both children were thirteen. Not believable but he never asked.

Both youngsters were athletic, and shiny with muscle and lean meat. Carlos and Tina.

Harry left them with the boat at the landing, and after the minute-long walk up to the house he tested the boards of the back porch, and tried the locked door. Now settled into the rocker which used to be his, boots up on the railing, he sucked in a deep breath of the familiar, still, riverine air. It felt good to lean back and pretend. But the grass needed cutting again and the clearing looked smaller, too, with the palmettos creeping back in closer each year. He sucked in a deep breath of the wild azaleas which he and Ivory had transplanted from the forest into the yard. They were in full bloom again — much larger now, of course — pink, orange, and yellow. The two pink bushes were hers, Ivory had always insisted, as if it made any difference. As if she needed to protect herself back in those happy days.

Bringing Briza's kids on this trip had been Harry's idea, but now he could hear their strident voices filtering up from the river. The thudding of the boat against the pier. The twangy clatter of an oar dropped in the hull. *What the hell are they doing?* He pictured their mother again. Would she be breaking for lunch now? Harry could see her. Pushing her maid's cart down the pretty but weedy walk past the apartment he rented behind the funky, old, beautiful motel at the southern edge of Florida City.

"Harry! The boat — is — leaking!" Tina was standing on the carefully raked sand bordering the porch, her sturdy, jean-legs spread in a wide stance, her chin up. She was staring at him over the railing as he jerked upright in the rocker.

"And the yellow-flies are biting us!" Her deep, throaty accent: "...bye-tin os!" Hands on her hips. Big, smart-ass eyes right on him. "Well?" Her short, yellow muscle-shirt poked out at him with accusing points.

Harry's boots clunked down onto the weathered porch-deck. "Leaking bad?"

"No. Not bad."

He watched her sprint back to the river path and disappear. The kids had seemed to enjoy the overnight trip to Apalachicola in his pickup. And the morning cruise up river was especially happy, a change from their precarious refuge within the ethnic milieu of

Florida City. They had pointed out everything to each other in rapid-fire Spanish: the turtles sunning on dead logs, the alligator sliding off the bank, the eddies and whirlpools where hidden tributaries joined the main stream. A belted kingfisher dropping out of the empty sky and bursting from the water with a silvery fish clamped in its lethal beak. And when they neared the landing — the first sign of human habitation for several miles — a bald eagle had powered up from a low perch directly over their heads.

When Harry caught up with her, the girl was dangling her legs off the end of the rickety pier and slapping flies. The boy was up to his knees beside the boat, the dark hairs showing through his wet undershorts, his dark skin glistening.

"Hey, gray beard! The plug thing is — busted. I take my hand away. See?"

Water boiled into the hull from the transom drain. Harry had to catch his balance as the pier shifted when he leaned over to look. That pier had been so sturdy when he built it. A present for Ivory when she had consented to move in with him here. Away from the reproaches, the frequently noisy challenges, that seemed to plague them in the city. "She ain' even finish school," her brothers would tell him. "You ol' honkey!"

"Well, Mister Harry, if I can' have no baby, so, maybe I can have a little pier here." Ivory, usually so quiet. So very tall and slow and graceful. "I could fish off it when you be on the job. When you be on the road."

"Hey, chief! What we do?"

Chief.... "We're stuck here," Harry said. "Stuck here till we starve to death. Old dude like me never knows what to do. No telephone. Food for only one day. We're dead, Carlito."

"Not me!" Tina said. "I figure out something!"

"She wants to be a whore when she grows up. A hoe."

"Yeah? You got a better idea, big brother?" Tina looked at Harry and touched the tip of her tongue to her upper lip. Then she blushed. "Fourteen. He think he is a man all ready! Mama says we all thirteen to piss everybody off. They look at Carlito and they say to me, 'Who is your father, girl?'" Tina spit into the river and the three of them watched the tiny island of foam hesitate, then begin to float downstream.

"You have so blue eyes, Harry," Tina said finally.

Carlos stared at him. "You fuck our mother?"

Harry pulled in a deep breath and looked from one to the other.

"He does!" Tina cried, her face beaming.

Carlos looked down and took his hand away from the transom drain and watched the water gush into the hull.

Tina said, "Is she good in bed?"

"Shut up, bitch! Maybe you have a different mother!"

"Okay, okay!" Harry shouted. "Tina, you take Carlito's place and hold your hand over the hole while we go and cut a plug. We'll need one that'll hold for our trip back."

"Huh!" Tina said. But she unbuttoned her 501's and began to tug the jeans down.

"No, wait!" Harry looked away.

"I no get my Levi's wet, thank you!"

"We can knot up a rag for now. Bottom's all mushy there. You don't want to stand in it."

But Carlos was already slogging toward the bank. "Mushy! Hurry, ho-sister, the boat is sinking!"

"Mushy," Tina repeated. The word must have sounded funny to them. Harry glanced at her just long enough to see she was wearing a bikini bottom. He heard her splash in. *So pretty....*

"Mushy! Don' worry! I handle it!"

"See? A hoe!"

"A virgin hoe!" Tina yelled.

"A virgin, illegal hoe!"

Harry looked up at the sun before starting up the path. Plenty of time, but the lack of sleep was beginning to tell on him. He heard more splashing and looked back. Carlos was at the end of the pier washing the mud off his legs.

"Be right with you!" He flicked his head back in Tina's direction. "Wet hoe T-shirt contest!"

"Not interested," Harry said quietly.

Carlos passed him on the path. He was barefoot, and still wearing the wet, see-through underwear briefs. Harry lowered his voice. Man-to-man. "We need to talk. Alone. We'll cut us a plug up here. There's a bench. See it?"

"Yeah. Sure. You own this?" Carlos waved his arm in a wide arc. "All this?"

"A long time ago. On paper I still do...." Harry placed a hand on the youth's smooth, cool shoulder. There was a time when he used to dream he would have another son one day. Start over. He would picture a tall, half-breed boy with bright blue eyes shining from a dark, happy face. A boy with many questions to ask. But Ivory, for some obscure, medical reason, would never be able to conceive.

He handed Carlos his knife and a short length of charred cypress. They sat, with a little distance between them, on the bench. "The cypress will swell when it gets wet. Makes a good plug."

"Flowers need water." Carlos pointed the knife at a small mound, planted with Cosmos and Impatiens.

"A little thinner. Then cut a taper."

"Taper?"

Harry explained. "That wood was in a fire." He saw the boy trying to rub clean his blackened palms. "We used to have a little love-nest on stilts over there. My second wife and me." He watched Carlos look at the blackened area, barely noticeable now and covered with wild ferns. Harry said, "She burned it down."

The young man worked silently for a time. Then he said, "She catch you porking some fox in there, huh, chief?"

"Something like that.... No, don't cut the end off yet. Hold it on the thin end and try cutting up." Harry could hear himself teaching but he couldn't stop. "Not so much taper. Easier if you hold the blade at an angle."

Carlos grunted, but he did as he was told. "She hot? Your girlfren'?"

Goose bumps rose on Harry's arms. "You're a smart-ass for fourteen, you know that?"

"She a blanca? A white girl? Foxy?" Carlos slumped a little and stopped carving. "We try it in the boat now? Maybe sister Heinz-57 Tina let the boat sink. Not as black as me. No paciencia. No — patience. You know."

"I know."

"So was your girlfren' white? Paint me a picture."

"I'm not going to tell you what color, Carlito. Maybe she was an alien. So what? Or a beautiful Viking...." Harry's heart cramped. He would call her "Teuton" sometimes, or "Sieglinde". She loved to take chances. And cheating on her husband.

"She loved guns," Harry said.

"A pistolera."

Harry had brought her out one day while Ivory was away visiting her parents. Hilda wanted to practice shooting right away. There was so much space and so many targets! Beer cans and bottles off the pilings at first, and suddenly a quick and sure swing-and-aim at the birdhouse Harry had helped Ivory build from a kit. The huge, .41 mag revolver bucking and twisting in Hilda's hands and the little home bursting in a yellow splatter of wood and feathers and tiny eggs. At that moment Harry knew he was selling out. The two of them hadn't yet worked out their lust for the day, and the destruction would go unpunished.

"The hoe is calling," Carlos said. "Hey! Chief!"

Harry shivered. "Don't call your sister a hoe, Carlito, okay? Not any lady. They have their dreams, too."

"Whatever you say, chief."

"That's what I wanted to say."

§

The three of them sat at the picnic table under the live oak up at the end of the clearing; the locked-up, frame house a sobering presence. Tina was passing out the sandwiches her mother had put together. "Oh, Harry! She put a beer in here for you. A Heineken. I think she loves you!" Tina laughed and handed him the cool, dripping, green bottle.

Harry felt under the table where a bottle opener was fastened to a brace, and accidentally clunked the bottle. *pschttt!* "Bless your mother. Bless Brizalita." He poured a dribble of beer onto the ground and raised the bottle to his lips.

"I hate that name, Briza." Tina held out her Pepsi. A can. "For my father, wherever is he."

"Whoever he is," Carlos said.

"Carlos, you look gross sitting in your underwear."

"You look gross sitting in that wet flea-market shirt. Fifty cents?" He raised his own Pepsi and touched it against Harry's bottle. "For my mother who is too young for you."

Tina covered her mouth. "Carlos!" She handed Harry a sandwich bag with his name on it. "Ham and cheese, no mayo. Carlos, here's your stupid corndog."

They ate, mostly in silence. Harry watching their skill at killing dog-flies. Yellow-flies. One slap, one dead fly. *Kids probably had to live outside at first. Who knows how they got to Florida. What Briza went through...* "How did you guys get in the country?" Harry tried to sound casual. He had asked their mother once and gotten a shrug.

Tina shrugged, and Carlos fished around in the cooler for another Ziploc with his name on it. "That was a long time ago."

Tina forced a laugh. "Don' seem like a long time for me!" She brushed a stray hair from her damp forehead. Thank you for the boat trip. We never go anywhere. So where is your dog?"

"It was my wife's dog. My second wife. Ivory's dog."

"Ivory!" Carlos shouted. "A-ha!"

"Shut up, Carlos! Harry, the picture of you holding him in your arms, your wife's dog? I can see the house here. On the mirror in your room. The only picture. You look happy in there."

"You saw my room?"

"Sure! I help Mama sometimes. You know, you hire a wetback, you get the whole family?"

Carlos was smiling. "Ivory's dog bark at your white girlfren'?"

Tina said, "What?" There was a hint of a mustache above her lip and it glistened with cola.

"Yip yip yip yip!" Carlos barked. He held out his right arm and made a pistol with his finger, pointing at nothing in particular, and cocked his thumb. "Boom!" His hand bucked up.

§

Carlos helped Harry drain the water tank at the well, then run the electric pump to charge the tank with air. Harry explained how it needed to be done at least twice a year. "The water in the tank dissolves the air over time. You need an air cushion." Then, surprising himself, he said, "I wish you were my son. You are a beautiful young man."

Tina trotted up. "Am I beautiful? Do you wish I am your daughter?"

"Yes, and I'd worry about you both, every minute."

"So hurry with the pump. I need water for those — wilty? — flowers over there. Is that a little grave?"

She stopped talking and covered her mouth. Maybe they had a little baby once. He had told her mother his children were all grown up and gone.

"We need to rake out our footprints before we leave," Harry said. "It's still early. We can let the boat drift downstream part of the way. See more wildlife that way. Plenty of time."

"You never drive here?"

"No.... Not anymore. It wouldn't seem right. People way down the road might see me, too, you know.... And I love the boat trip."

When they were whisking away their footprints from the sandy patches in the clearing, Carlos turned and looked again at the little flower bed his half-sister had watered. The plants were standing proud now, and they looked happy. He pointed a finger at them and pressed his lips together.

Silently, his hand bucked up into the air. •

Bible School Tattoo

I was alone and hoping for some cash business when the couple strolled up, hesitant but holding hands and laughing. Black T-shirts and faded jeans. Before they came in they looked over the pictures in my storefront window. Some of my past work looking its best in the bright glow of the afternoon light streaming down our funky, South Florida street. No hard-core stuff pinned up there, though. Some big color prints of bikers and their mamas, and a great shot of my old lady, who is a beautiful, tall, sexy-looking girl — a woman more-or-less devoted and faithful to me. In the picture I am so proud of, Paula is turned to one side with one hand hiking up the skirt of her nurse's uniform to show this cute mouse tattooed on her chunky-little, bare bottom, the mouse heading for the dark safety of its home. The natives and the tourists alike stop and gawk at this one. I love that picture, I love the tattoo, and I love Paula.

The couple finally made it in and I caught a whiff of their perfume, his and hers, male and female. Not too much and very civilized — the scent, not the looks of them. I had already turned on the hot-plate for the coffee I would be needing, and was leaning back in my rocking chair and scoping them out. People are afraid of AIDS now so I knew what their first question would be. But they just stood there, still holding hands, and giggling.

I nodded toward a couch. "Want to sit down? Talk it over?"

We are in the Florida Keys and our parlor looks like an airy but clean, 1960's crash-pad: old, deep couches, colorful rag-rugs on a Cuban tile floor, a jungle of indoor and outdoor plants, plenty of bright, jalousie windows wide-open to the beautiful fall weather, a huge black & white poster of Ho Chi Minh, when he was about eighty years old, with a lighted Salem cigarette protruding from his delicate, aged fingers....

The female released her grip on her companion's hand and picked a seat as close to me as she could. I thought I recognized her from a picture on the front page of a religious booklet some well-meaning local had jammed under the door a while back. "Soldiers for Christ" I think they called themselves. In the group photo, this particular god-trooper had the top three buttons of her blouse open and I remember finding that peculiar. Being a seasoned dude, I am aware that ladies always know exactly how many buttons are unbuttoned.

The girl was attractive but possibly underage. Maybe I'd seen that face on a milk carton?

"We've been drinking a little," she smiled. Her eyes caught mine when my gaze returned to her face. "Are your needles clean? Sterilized?"

The boyfriend butted in. "Is that a real nurse in that picture in the window? Does she work here?"

"Yup. She's all mine. I think.... We're legal now — finally got married. She works at the hospital and has to keep her nursing license up-to-date. Anyway, we keep everything sterilized. Besides, the health inspector raids the place without warning whenever he gets bored with slipping on fresh turds on nursing home floors. We always pass — you came to the right place."

They mumbled to each other and giggled again. The teakettle whistled and I got up to fix my instant — some of the brown powder already cementing itself to the wet spots on my counter. The female was so pretty! I began to hope the tattoo they wanted was fated to embellish a breast. Perhaps a milk-loving butterfly.... So boring and ho-hum but those mothy critters frequently keep the pot boiling — for this artist, anyway. Like what painting sailboats-on-the-bay is to brush-jockeys who sell to tourists, except they don't get to palpate this bewitching, warm object plump in the hand while they're fletching out the obligatory pelican on the old wharf piling. When Paula is home (we live behind the shop) she does the tits. We have that sort of agreement. Not out of jealousy, either. I've tried doing it with her there but it blows my mind and I can't concentrate with Paula watching while I'm trying to tame this precious, sweet item, pinching the skin tight for the needle, the forbidden fruit speaking to me the whole time. And wanting to jump Paula's bones after the job is done — Paula knowing that my hands-on encounter with another female is what aroused the old reptile. I digress....

I was making a big deal of stirring my coffee, not wanting to push anything. And I was happy the couple had been boozing it up a little, alcohol being a prerequisite for newcomers to the tattooist's art.

"We made a bet and, uhhh...." The girl couldn't finish.

I was nodding. I have tattooed the multitudes over the years: winners and losers of bets. I put down my coffee cup and reached into the table-top fridge for a Corona.

"Beer?"

They both thought it over, then shook their heads. The girl sucked in a deep breath and looked me in the eye. "Larry says that Mark Twain, you know — he wrote Tom Sawyer and Huckleberry Finn?" She noted my look of disappointment and didn't understand it. "Well, this has to do with our bet!"

"Okay, go ahead!"

"Anyway, Larry was saying that when the Great Flood came, all the diseases on earth had to be given to Noah's family, and all the animal diseases to the animals, you know, because they needed to survive, too. The diseases, I mean. The bugs."

Larry interrupted with a loud laugh. "After forty days and forty nights, the ark was a boat-load of slime!"

"One hundred fifty days," the girl said.

Larry reached for the beer and I got out another one for her, successfully squashing the timid voice in my head that had been questioning her age. But I made them figure out they'd need an opener.

She continued. "We were in this bar when we made the bet and they told us that yours was the place to go to because you used to be a preacher. The guy playing the piano knows you. Barry Cuda."

"Oh, yeah, Barry! Cuda's not his real last name, but...."

Larry jerked a thumb in the girl's direction. "Judy used to go into bars and invite people to her church!" Larry was grinning a mouthful of bright teeth. "Then she met me, ha ha!"

"Preacher, huh?" I said. "No, but my father was, and his father! Yup.... So you want a tattoo of the ark."

"No," Larry said. "That's not the bet."

"The bet is," Judy said slowly, "that if Mark Twain was right — if all the diseases of the human race ..."

Larry interrupted. "Twain said if all the names of all the diseases God wanted to preserve on the ark were printed on a man's body, there'd be so many you wouldn't be able to see the man! Even if you printed them all as small as possible!"

They looked at me. Neither of them could get the caps of their beer bottles so I did it for them. "The secret's using this bottle opener," I said. "So I still don't understand your bet. I don't think that's in Tom Sawyer or Huck Finn, anyway. I read them both. A long time ago, but this I would remember!" I was amused. I'd never thought about the ark that way but it certainly seemed more reasonable than the antiseptic version I was fed as a lad in Sunday school.

Larry was quick to add color to my new picture. "All those poor animals sick, and puking up kernel-corn! And Noah's family too nauseated to mop it up!"

"And diarrhea!" Judy said.

"And no Palestinians to clean it up for them!" I added. But it was time to get down to business. "I know. You want me to tattoo a dove bringing in an olive branch."

"Bringing in a shovel! Larry laughed. "No, Judy bet there weren't that many names of diseases to cover up a person's skin from head to toe, but everybody in the bar said there probably was so Judy agreed that if we can figure out how much space it would take to print as many as possible, as small as possible, that if there are any names left over, the very next disease gets tattooed on her ass!"

"Inside the bikini line," Judy was quick to add.

Ah, the life of tatt! I got up and looked over the shelf of medical and tattoo books Paula and I displayed to improve the unprofessional look of the rest of the studio. I wished she were there just then, too — she would have loved this! And I missed her, and wondered where she was. I wished I'd told her I loved her when she left that morning.

"This manual has every disease known to man," I said, handing a heavy volume to Larry. "Nothing on animals, though, I don't think. Make a rough count from the index. Here, use this little calculator." I handed him that while Judy rose up to look over his shoulder. "And we'll need to know the average length of a disease, you know, the average number of letters. Paula knows more about this stuff than I do. She's a preacher's kid, too. That's how we got together, in fact — that's what broke the ice for us when we met — talking about our PK childhoods. She's rare. A true, Florida native! Actually born in Key West! Her mother even waited until the sunset was over!"

They were both looking at me rather sympathetically, and smiling. I shut off the enthusiasm and pulled out the very first book on tattooing I ever owned. Printed in Hong Kong. It gave the skin area of a human being in good, old-fashioned, non-metric square-inches.

An hour and a six-pack later found all three of us totally fascinated with Larry's discoveries. "And this book only covers bugs found in the United States!" he was saying. "And since most of them had to have a host, you know, to survive the Great Flood, oh, this is so beautiful!"

Larry was a full-blown heathen, I figured, but Judy seemed to wince at every remark critical of her parents' religion. Oh, well, I was going to get to tattoo her ass. Who am I to question God's will?

"Look! Look at this!" Larry shouted, holding up the book with about fifty pages pinched together. "This section is just about parasitic worms!"

"It's a cruel world."

"Believe it!"

"No names of worms," Judy said. "I insist on that."

"Listen to this! Borrelia burgdorferi! Lyme disease! That tick-borne shit. Says here the germ is related to Treponema Pallidium, the syphilis bug, which has — get this! — eight to fourteen little spiral, corkscrew things which it twists and rotates. The germ screws its way right through your meat!"

"The Father's works are great," I said. I was missing Paula more than ever. She would have been into this discussion with both feet, and with a lot more marbles to bring to the table.

"Satan must've created that stuff," Judy said.

"Satin created nothing," I reminded her. "Sorry, but the Bible says God made everything." Judy looked so sweet, so fine, so delectable. And wounded. "It's not so bad, Judy. Faith and inquiry are always..."

Larry couldn't wait. "Besides, who created Satan? So — so what!" His head was bent into the book. "Check this out! Clostridium sporogenes! You know how I found this gem? I closed the book, shut my eyes, and opened it to a random page. I allowed for Divine Guidance! Listen! This wondrous little speck of life, when it gets on you, it liquefies your meat. It digests your tissue! Woe!"

"We need to get into the average number of letters per name," I reminded them. "Calculate if all the names will fit on Judy, if they will, and if they won't we need to calculate where in the index we'll have to stop. Where her body would be full, so to speak." *Did they really think I was serous? About calculating all this?!* "My book here gives the skin area for an average Asian — well, that might be close to Judy's size.... Agreed?" I sighed. I was suddenly getting bored, and having switched from coffee to Corona to Michelob somewhere back there, I was getting a buzz, too. Not too drunk to do the tattoo, but too far gone to do the calculations. So were they. Suddenly, without any trouble at all, we decided that the name of the disease destined to grace Judy's divine, little bottom should be:

LARRY

Larry did not relish watching me pinch up Judy's cheek to keep the lettering straight, and he went out for another six-pack. He was back and sitting near the front door when Paula finally appeared. Judy's jeans were draped over my rocking chair and her bikini panties were hanging from an arm — clothing which she had jettisoned with amazing zeal. I was just finishing up, zinging in the final "Y" when Paula peered over my shoulder for a moment, her long hair hanging down and brushing my grizzled neck.

"LARRY", I said.

I tried to explain by starting out at the beginning of the whole, joyous story. Paula helped me tape a sterile 4X4 bandage over the work and Judy eased down from our padded table. While she jerked and tried to tug on tight jeans over her panties, I gave her instructions on how to handle any temporary scabbing. Paula handed them our card with the shop's phone number, and gave Larry a hard look.

"I hope you two are a permanent team."

I laughed. "You guys are lucky. Paula usually insists on equal treatment — the girl's name on the boyfriend's ass." I was anxious for them to leave now. I was horny, and Paula looked so foxy and alive. She was counting out the pile of crumpled bills they had forked over — mostly singles.

"Larry's been getting into male stripping over at the Mas-0-Keys-Mo Club," Judy explained. "Just part-time, though,"

Real aristocrats. I watched Paula look up and give Larry a more thorough appraisal. I wondered if she ever stopped in at that joint and if she would stick one-dollar bills into Larry's jock-string.

Larry had indolently sprawled himself out on the couch and Paula plunked down beside him. "You shouldn't make fun of Judy's religion," she said with a straight face.

"Whoa! Paula? Is that you?" I tried to stare down her dark eyes which had suddenly turned on me. I knew it was time to shut up but I couldn't help myself. The truth is the truth. "Didn't you just tell me the other day you physically shoved Reverend Pitts out of the Emergency room?"

"Preacher Pitts? Hell, yes! Old Pick-and-Choose I called him, too! That's all they're good for, picking what they like out of their book and ignoring all the rest!"

"Right on, nurse!" Larry shouted. "Burn 'em! Give 'em hell!"

One last look at Paula's livid face and I settled back into my own chair for the inevitable sermon.

"Preachers! At the hospital they come barging into the ER while we're trying to save some car-crash victim or whatever — bleeding to fucking death and choking on their own puke — and in comes the God Squad to pray and get in the way. I shove them right back out through those double doors! I yell at them! I mean, I scream I get so mad! I say, like, "Is The Lord going to save this patient or are we?!"

Larry sat up a little and clapped his hands. "Aw right!"

Paula clenched a fist and punched Larry above the knee. "Listen to this! One night they brought this little three-year-old in. Cancer. The family had planned to let the little guy spend his last days at home but he was suffering so, and choking, and they were desperate for help. We had to suction and tube him and give him a shot of morphine. Then in comes the family preacher, wouldn't you know, just like clockwork, and I told him, I said, "I want your boss's phone number! Now! This poor, precious little boy — look at him! Even a fucking lawnmower comes with a warranty!"

"Yeah!" Larry said, nodding his head vigorously. Judy was still standing, quietly patting her ass through her jeans and studying the pictures of our work on the wall.

Paula wasn't finished. "And when these fundamentalists get sick and it's their turn to go? Ha! They demand every procedure known to medical science to prolong their life here on this earth. They beg us! They can whip out their Medicaid cards faster than they can unzip their Bibles! They want to be operated on again! Do they have insurance? Hell no! 'God will provide', they say. I yell at them, 'You mean the government will provide! Taxpayers! People who work! People like me! For what?! Don't you want to be reunited with the Lord you're always telling us about? If you die don't you go to Heaven?'"

Paula was in fine form. I was so proud and so much in love with her that tears were welling up.

Judy had moved to the door, looking bored and impatient. Thank God or whatever, Larry finally remembered her and got up. But Paula had his real attention.

"The hospital doesn't fire you for stuff like that?"

"Oh, they did eventually, but I still work there part-time." Paula grinned. "There's a nurse shortage around here."

"No shortage of diseases, misery, and death!" Larry said happily, as he and Judy finally made it out. "That's gospel!"

We were alone. I went over and gave my lady a long, lingering, Anheuser-Busch hug. (I wouldn't trade her for two, golden Cubans, as we like to say in South Florida). "I know one thing for sure. There's..."

Paula interrupted. She was still on the pulpit. "Only preachers know anything for sure!"

"Yeah, well, I know for sure there's a shortage of nurses as beautiful and wild as you." I patted her ass over the mouse headed for home. I had to pat her gently. My name was over that mouse — for a couple days now — and the lettering hadn't quite healed. •

THE END

JOHN AALBORG

For ordering and publishing information contact
Bleep-Free Press
http://bleepfreepress.com

References for "Bible School Tattoo":
• Genesis 7:19-24
• Letters from the Earth — Mark Twain,
  Bernard DeVoto (Harper & Row 1962)

Books by John Aalborg:
Novels, *plus this short story collection:*
>   Harry & Ivory
>   Lowboy #22
>   Children of The Lambs
>   *Gulf Coast Stories*
Self help with attitude:
>   666 Words — Meditations